RIPPLE EFFECT

LANTERN BEACH BLACKOUT, BOOK 3

CHRISTY BARRITT

Copyright © 2020 by Christy Barritt

All rights reserved.

No part of this book may be reproduced in any form or by any electronic or mechanical means, including information storage and retrieval systems, without written permission from the author, except for the use of brief quotations in a book review.

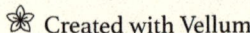 Created with Vellum

COMPLETE BOOK LIST

Squeaky Clean Mysteries:
- #1 Hazardous Duty
- #2 Suspicious Minds
- #2.5 It Came Upon a Midnight Crime (novella)
- #3 Organized Grime
- #4 Dirty Deeds
- #5 The Scum of All Fears
- #6 To Love, Honor and Perish
- #7 Mucky Streak
- #8 Foul Play
- #9 Broom & Gloom
- #10 Dust and Obey
- #11 Thrill Squeaker
- #11.5 Swept Away (novella)
- #12 Cunning Attractions

#13 Cold Case: Clean Getaway
#14 Cold Case: Clean Sweep
#15 Cold Case: Clean Break
#16 Cleans to an End (coming soon)
While You Were Sweeping, A Riley Thomas Spinoff

The Sierra Files:
#1 Pounced
#2 Hunted
#3 Pranced
#4 Rattled

The Gabby St. Claire Diaries (a Tween Mystery series):
The Curtain Call Caper
The Disappearing Dog Dilemma
The Bungled Bike Burglaries

The Worst Detective Ever
#1 Ready to Fumble
#2 Reign of Error
#3 Safety in Blunders
#4 Join the Flub
#5 Blooper Freak
#6 Flaw Abiding Citizen

#7 Gaffe Out Loud
#8 Joke and Dagger
#9 Wreck the Halls
#10 Glitch and Famous (coming soon)

Raven Remington
Relentless 1
Relentless 2 (coming soon)

Holly Anna Paladin Mysteries:
#1 Random Acts of Murder
#2 Random Acts of Deceit
#2.5 Random Acts of Scrooge
#3 Random Acts of Malice
#4 Random Acts of Greed
#5 Random Acts of Fraud
#6 Random Acts of Outrage
#7 Random Acts of Iniquity

Lantern Beach Mysteries
#1 Hidden Currents
#2 Flood Watch
#3 Storm Surge
#4 Dangerous Waters
#5 Perilous Riptide
#6 Deadly Undertow

Lantern Beach Romantic Suspense
Tides of Deception
Shadow of Intrigue
Storm of Doubt
Winds of Danger
Rains of Remorse

Lantern Beach P.D.
On the Lookout
Attempt to Locate
First Degree Murder
Dead on Arrival
Plan of Action

Lantern Beach Escape
Afterglow (a novelette)

Lantern Beach Blackout
Dark Water
Safe Harbor
Ripple Effect
Rising Tide

Carolina Moon Series
Home Before Dark
Gone By Dark

Wait Until Dark
Light the Dark
Taken By Dark

Suburban Sleuth Mysteries:
Death of the Couch Potato's Wife

Fog Lake Suspense:
Edge of Peril
Margin of Error
Brink of Danger
Line of Duty

Cape Thomas Series:
Dubiosity
Disillusioned
Distorted

Standalone Romantic Mystery:
The Good Girl

Suspense:
Imperfect
The Wrecking

Sweet Christmas Novella:

Home to Chestnut Grove

Standalone Romantic-Suspense:
Keeping Guard
The Last Target
Race Against Time
Ricochet
Key Witness
Lifeline
High-Stakes Holiday Reunion
Desperate Measures
Hidden Agenda
Mountain Hideaway
Dark Harbor
Shadow of Suspicion
The Baby Assignment
The Cradle Conspiracy
Trained to Defend

Nonfiction:
Characters in the Kitchen
Changed: True Stories of Finding God through Christian Music (out of print)
The Novel in Me: The Beginner's Guide to Writing and Publishing a Novel (out of print)

CHAPTER ONE

BETHANY MCINTYRE WATCHED as her daughter, Ada, ran into a tunnel in the play area. Her daughter's friend Luke chased her, and giggles of delight escaped from both of them.

Something about having her three-year-old out of sight, even if only for a few seconds, always made Bethany tense. With an ex-husband who'd fought the world's most violent and deadly people as a Navy SEAL, the harsh realities of life had always seemed too close at hand for Bethany, more so than the average person.

"Aren't they just adorable?" Bethany's friend Cindi said as they stood beside each other, monitoring this kiddie wonderland.

The two of them worked together at *Engineering*

Plus Magazine. They'd brought their kids to a park that had just opened today in Virginia Beach. That had been their first mistake. Everybody else in town had the same idea. Not only was the park new, but the May weather was perfect.

The playground was state of the art with multiple bridges, towers, and climbing walls. An area with colorful obstacles graced one side, and at least six slides looped from various platforms. The whole area was surrounded by a thin line of woods, a pond, and a Japanese garden. Mix that with the scents of freshly cut grass and popcorn from a nearby vendor, and it was nearly perfect.

"Adorable?" Bethany smiled, remembering her friend's observation about their kids. "Yes. A handful? Also yes."

Bethany and Cindi laughed together. This was the period of parenthood that left the most able-bodied moms and dads exhausted. Besides that, a bad feeling had lingered in Bethany's gut all day, and she had no idea why. She'd probably been watching the news too much lately. That always made her more suspicious of people and caused her to look for trouble around every corner.

Cindi put her hands on her hips as she stared at the kids around them. Cindi was several years older than Bethany. She hadn't gotten married until she was thirty-five, and she'd had Luke two years later. The woman had short blonde hair, stood at nearly six feet tall, and carried about forty extra pounds on her since having Luke.

"I don't know how you do it as a single mom, but you make it look easy," Cindi muttered.

"You're being too kind." Bethany's eyes remained on the tunnel. She saw Ada run by a window on the side and breathed a little easier. The line between caution and paranoia was thin and wrought with potential breaches, it seemed.

"You're the type who handles anything life throws at you with a good dose of grace. Me? I run out of coffee in the morning, and my whole day is ruined. First world problems, right?"

"I've had plenty of experience tapping into that grace." Bethany wished she was joking, but she wasn't. The past couple years had been trying at best. Life today looked nothing like she'd envisioned, but she was making the best of things.

Bethany waited to see Ada emerge from the tunnel.

She still hadn't come out.

Familiar worry filled her again.

You're at a playground, Bethany. There's nothing to be concerned about.

"So, you talk to Mason anymore?" Cindi asked before popping a cheese-flavored cracker—one of Luke's snacks—into her mouth.

Bethany glanced up in surprise. "My neighbor?"

"Who else?"

Bethany shook her head, the question throwing her off guard. "Mason is just a friend."

"He'd like to be more." Cindi wiggled her eyebrows. "I've seen the way he looks at you."

"I'm not interested." Bethany shrugged and kept her attention focused on the play area. She really didn't want to talk about this, but she knew her friend meant well.

"Not ready to date again, huh?"

Bethany didn't tell her friend that ending her marriage to Griff had torn her heart in half. She still wasn't over her grief. Not even close. "I just want to focus on Ada."

"Makes sense."

Bethany released her breath when she saw Ada run out of the tunnel. With a huge, sloppy grin on her face, Ada darted to Bethany and wrapped her arms around her mama's legs. Ada let out a little squeal as five-year-old Luke chased her. The boy's arms were raised as if he were a T-Rex.

"You didn't let him catch you?" Bethany said. "Good girl."

Ada giggled before running off again. Luke followed, and Bethany's momentary relief was replaced with familiar apprehension.

Bethany would much rather hold Ada's hand and keep her close. But she knew that wasn't always possible. Children needed some freedom to explore—under supervision, of course.

Ada was like her dad. She liked her independence, and she liked to do things her way.

At the thought of Griff, Bethany's smile disappeared. It was better if she didn't think about her ex. All that ever brought was heartache.

Had they really been separated for a year now? Sometimes, it felt like decades, and other times mere weeks. The divorce papers had been filed, and she was waiting to get the official documents back. She'd been told it could take up to a month.

Bethany moved along the perimeter of the space to keep a better eye on her daughter. As she did, Ada climbed some stairs toward a bridge, and Bethany lost sight of her again. Her heart rate quickened.

She's going to come running out here anytime now, Luke behind her with his T-Rex arms raised.

Bethany waited.

Still no Ada. No Luke.

Her heart beat faster.

Anytime now, she told herself.

Still not yet.

"Where did they go?" Cindi scanned the crowds.

"I'm sure we'll spot them any minute now." Bethany's voice sounded strained, as if she doubted her own words.

But she still didn't see the kids, and her anxiety continued to rise.

Luke came down a slide and ran toward them. "Mommy, where's Ada?"

"You were chasing her." Cindi bent toward him. "You tell me."

"I think she may have hidden from me. Sometimes she likes to play hide-and-seek."

Ada was only three. Bethany knew she could only expect so much from the preschooler. But playing hide-and-go-seek in a public area set Bethany's worry over the edge.

"Ada!" she called.

Bethany wandered between the slides and under

the bridge and peered around to the other side of the tower.

No Ada.

Panic started to swell in Bethany until her head spun. Certainly, she was overthinking this. At any minute now, Ada would appear.

They would hug. Everything would be okay. Bethany would insist that they leave and get some ice cream, just to get away from these crowds.

Beyond the tower, Bethany still didn't see her daughter.

"No sign of her yet?" Cindi put another cracker in her mouth. "It's so strange. How far away could she have gotten?"

"Good question."

"Ms. Bethany! Over there!" Luke pointed toward the perimeter of the park, toward the back where the trees were.

Ada . . .

A man walked beside her daughter, leading her away from the playground.

A man Bethany had never seen before.

She *wasn't* being paranoid.

Bethany sprinted toward her daughter, her muscles burning under the strain.

There was no time to waste. If that man left with Ada, Bethany might never see her again.

Just then, the man glanced back. His eyes widened when he saw Bethany. The next instant, he lifted Ada into his arms.

"No!" Bethany pushed her legs faster. "Ada!"

She couldn't let that man leave with her daughter.

Bethany saw the chain-link fence in the distance, beyond the trees at the edge of the property. It had to be at least seven feet high.

What would the man do? Try to scale it with Ada?

Bethany pushed herself forward. She couldn't make up the distance between them. She was fast, but not that fast. Still, she had to try.

Footsteps sounded behind her. People yelled.

Time seemed to slow.

The man glanced back again.

Bethany's heart slammed into her ribcage, each beat causing an ache.

What was he going to do? She prayed he wouldn't hurt her daughter.

The man glanced at Ada once more then back at the people running toward him. He hadn't expected to be caught, had he?

At once, he set Ada on the ground. Then he hopped over the fence and disappeared from sight.

Bethany reached Ada and scooped her daughter up in her arms. She held Ada close. Felt those chubby arms around her. Smelled that honey-scented hair.

She was never letting her daughter go. Never.

"I HATE SURFING!" Griff McIntyre yelled over the roar of the waves.

He'd managed to stand up on the surfboard, but he felt unsteady. Being at the mercy of the ocean made him feel like life was out of control. He'd always hated that feeling.

"You're a former Navy SEAL," Benjamin James yelled back. He was on the surfboard next to Griff's, but he looked much more comfortable than Griff in his wetsuit. "Nothing is supposed to scare you."

"I didn't say it scared me. I just said I didn't like it."

"Wuss," Benjamin said.

"Takes one to know one."

"Real mature!"

That was the last thing Griff remembered

hearing before he wiped out. He tumbled beneath the water then surfaced among the tumultuous waves. Grabbing his board, he swam the rest of the way to shore. He was ready for a break from his surfing lesson.

It was May, and tourist season was about to hit hard in Lantern Beach, North Carolina. So far this week, Griff had no assignments for his job with Blackout, a private security firm that operated out of Lantern Beach, so he planned on enjoying a bit of the beach life.

He plopped down on his beach towel and gave his friends Colton Locke and Dez Rodriguez a scowl as they glanced his way.

"Not a word," he muttered.

"Who said we were going to say anything?" Dez rubbed some sunscreen on his shoulders.

"You don't have to. I can see it in your eyes. You're both judging me."

"I thought you looked good out there." Colton's words lacked sincerity, and he covered his smile by taking a sip of his water—a long sip.

"And by looking good, he means looking good for a total amateur." Dez chuckled.

Aggravation was their preferred means of communication off the job. It always had been. Griff brushed them off and reached into his bag to grab some cherries he'd packed. They were his favorite oceanside snack, and they reminded him of his Michigan roots.

As he popped one in his mouth, his phone rang.

He stiffened when he saw the name on the screen.

Bethany McIntyre.

He hadn't talked to his ex in at least two months. She'd made it clear last time that she had no desire to ever speak with him again. So why was she calling now?

"Excuse me." Griff gripped his phone and walked away from any listening ears before answering. "Bethany. What's going on?"

Griff tried to keep his voice casual. It was always a struggle. Because casual was never something he felt around Bethany. No, he felt invigorated. Infatuated. Infuriated.

But never casual.

"It's Ada." Bethany's voice sounded breathless and scratchy.

Everything else faded from around Griff. Had his daughter been in an accident? Was she sick? "What happened to Ada?"

"Someone tried to snatch her today. At the park."

Bethany's voice broke, turning into a barely contained sob.

"Is she okay?" Griff rushed. "Did they catch the guy who did this?"

Bethany sucked in a shaky breath before she continued. "She's okay. I don't think she fully understands what happened. The police didn't catch this guy, though. I don't know what to do or where to go from here."

"Did you get a good look at him?"

"He was wearing a hat and sunglasses. It was hard to really see him. But I gave his description to the police, and they're looking into it."

Griff's heart pounded in his ears. He drew in a deep breath, trying to temper his reaction. But the very thought of what had happened caused white-hot anger to surge through his blood.

"Bethany . . . I'm so sorry."

"Me too." She paused. "But there's more."

"What is it?" More tension roiled in Griff's stomach as he waited to hear what she had to say next. How could this get much worse?

"A car pulled away from the scene. Someone nearby got the license plate. Apparently, the man who owns it has been linked to a terrorist group. Maybe you've heard of them. The Savages?"

As soon as Griff heard their name, the blood drained from his face, and he froze. All he could hear was the thumping of his heart.

No . . . this couldn't be happening.

He licked his lips and turned away from the glaring sun. "The Savages?"

"That's what the police said. Apparently, this guy is on one of those most-wanted lists. I don't know. It's all a blur."

Griff's jaw tightened as he stared across the water, his mind racing. These guys were targeting his family, weren't they? The group had been quiet over the past few months, but Griff should have known that was too good to be true. In their silence, they'd been plotting their next move.

"Where are you now, Bethany?"

"I'm at my condo. Why?"

"I need you and Ada to come here. To Lantern Beach."

"Why would we want to do that? This whole thing was random. Right?"

He wanted to believe that, but he couldn't. He'd seen what these guys were capable of. Death. Destruction. Darkness. "I don't know. But you're not safe there."

Bethany paused, and the sound of her breathing filled the line. "Griff, you're scaring me."

"You should be scared. I mean it, Bethany. You're not safe. Ada's not safe."

"I . . . I just can't leave everything."

Griff ran a hand over his face, reminding himself to stay calm. He had to convince Bethany to come here with Ada. He would go get them himself, but there was no time for that. If the Savages didn't get what they wanted the first time, they would try again.

"You can take leave from work, right?" he asked.

"Yes, I guess . . ."

"Perfect. I can arrange a place for you to stay and people to keep an eye on you. At least until we know what's going on. Please, Bethany. Don't argue with me on this one. I wouldn't ask this if I wasn't concerned."

She didn't say anything for a minute, and Griff waited, fully expecting her to refuse. She had every right to be angry with him. But with Ada's safety on the line, they needed to put that behind them and do what was best for their daughter.

Finally, Bethany said, "Okay. Fine. I'll come to Lantern Beach."

Relief filled Griff. But only for a minute. Having

them here would allow Griff to keep an eye on Bethany and Ada. But that didn't mean their troubles were over. No, not by a long shot.

After they discussed her arrival, Griff ended the call and stared at the ocean for another minute. He needed a plan.

Because there was no way he would let anything happen to his little girl... or to Bethany.

CHAPTER TWO

BETHANY PARKED her car under a stilted house on Hatteras Island, just as Griff had instructed her to do. Apparently, he knew the owner, who'd approved of them meeting here.

It had taken Bethany almost three hours to travel this far. She'd only taken enough time to grab some necessary items and call her boss before hitting the road.

Griff had made it clear this was urgent. He'd sounded like he wanted to come to Virginia Beach himself to pick her and Ada up, but they'd both realized that would take too much time. Instead, they'd agreed to meet halfway.

She swallowed hard and glanced around her. No

one appeared to be at the two-story beach house. No cars were parked in the driveway, at least.

That didn't stop Bethany from feeling like eyes were nearby, watching and waiting. That bad feeling she'd had all day remained—the sense that she was the prey and that a predator was just waiting to make another move.

She glanced back at Ada. Her daughter snoozed in the backseat, head resting against the polka-dotted car seat cover. Though the pink material looked sweet and girly, the marker streaks on the fabric confirmed that her daughter had a feisty side.

Bethany glanced at her watch. Griff should be here any minute.

She let out a long breath, trying to keep her emotions in check in the meantime. Panicking wouldn't do any good right now. Instead, she began gathering her trash from their journey—leftover bags of grapes, juice boxes, some stray French fries—Bethany's guilty pleasure and a last-minute splurge on the way here.

Bethany's head still spun as she thought about everything that happened. It seemed surreal that she was here, that she was doing this. But Ada had almost been abducted today. Bethany couldn't be in denial about that.

Maybe this remote island that was only accessible by ferry would keep them safe for a while. She'd heard so much about the place.

Bethany wasn't committing to stay for any lengthy amount of time. Maybe just a couple days until she could get her head back on her shoulders. Until they could find some answers.

She glanced in the backseat and saw Ada still sleeping soundly.

Her little girl looked so much like Griff with her sparkling eyes, unwavering courage, and blonde hair that fell all around her face, giving her an almost angelic look.

The angelic part she definitely did *not* get from her father. Griff had been more of the bad boy. Bethany had been convinced that she could reform Griff into the committed type.

That had been Bethany's first mistake, and her parents would never let her live that down.

But even if their marriage had been a mistake, Ada was anything but. Bethany loved this little girl like nothing else in this world.

The muscles in Bethany's shoulders tensed as she heard a car coming down the gravel lane. A moment later, a black truck pulled into the driveway.

Her heart throbbed in her ears as she saw Griff

step out and stride toward her like the brooding hero he was. That confidence had been the first thing that attracted Bethany to him.

Why did that man still have this effect on her? Bethany assumed with all the problems that they had, she'd feel nothing but contempt toward the man. But that would be too easy.

She observed him for a moment. Griff McIntyre was tall with broad shoulders and thick arms. His blond hair was a little too long. Right now, he wore a tank top with some cutoff shorts and flip-flops. His aviator sunglasses completed his look, making him appear intimidating and coolly in control.

"Bethany . . ." Griff paused in front of her. He almost looked like he was about to say something sweet, like she looked good. Instead, he said, "You look tired."

She felt her shoulders deflate, even if just a little. His opinion didn't matter, she reminded herself. "I am."

He either didn't notice her irritation or didn't care. "Did anybody follow you here?"

"No. I kept watch, just like you said. I didn't see anyone."

"Good." He pulled his sunglasses up on the top

of his head as his gaze drifted in through the window to Ada. His eyes softened.

It was clear to anybody watching just how much he cared about his little girl. So why didn't Griff want to be a part of Ada's life? It made no sense, and Bethany had nothing but time to think about it for the past year.

As if Ada had sensed Griff was near, the girl's eyes popped open. Her gaze lit up with equal parts delight and surprise when she spotted her father.

"Daddy!" She reached her chubby hands out. "Daddy, Daddy, Daddy!"

Griff's entire face beamed with adoration as he opened her door. "How's Daddy's girl?"

"Good, Daddy." Ada kicked her legs with excitement. "Daddy, can we have a tea party? Please."

"A tea party? Who doesn't want to have a tea party? Drinking out of little cups while raising your pinky is one of the highlights of life."

Griff fiddled with Ada's seatbelt, and, a moment later, Ada was free and in her dad's very capable arms. The two embraced each other, looking like the picture of happiness.

Seeing Griff hold Ada, seeing the bond they still had despite their time apart made Bethany's heart pound with regret. Her life was not supposed to turn out this way. Her little girl was supposed to have the happy family upbringing Bethany had.

But this wasn't the time to feel sorry for herself. Right now, all Bethany needed to think about was keeping her daughter safe. Nothing else mattered—not even the strong dislike she felt toward Griff.

"Come on." Griff turned back to Bethany, as if he'd just then remembered she was here. "You can leave your car here. I cleared it with my friend who owns this place. I'll drive you back to Lantern Beach."

Bethany hesitated for long enough that Griff paused and gave her a look.

"What?" His eyebrows shoved together. "Do you think I'm going to trap you on the island with no means of getting back home on your own?"

The thought *had* crossed her mind. But she knew Griff better than that. He was many things, but he was not vindictive.

"Let me just get our things from the trunk." Bethany tried to keep her voice perky in order not to alarm Ada.

She popped the trunk. It was packed full, with suitcases, three bags of Ada-approved food, and uncountable other things.

"I can see you still like to pack light," Griff commented drily, his eyebrows flicking up.

Bethany crossed her arms, already tired of his ribbing—and she'd just gotten here. "Very funny. We don't have to do this."

He held up his hand. "Calm down. I'm just giving you a hard time."

Still holding Ada in one arm, he scooped down and picked up some bags to transfer to the back of his truck. Bethany helped until everything had been transferred over.

Griff gave Ada one more kiss on her chubby little cheek before handing her to Bethany. "Let me get the car seat situated and then we'll be all set to go, Warrior Princess."

Warrior Princess. That's what Griff always called Ada. He'd said he couldn't raise her to be a damsel in distress. She was stronger than that.

It was one thing Bethany and Griff had agreed on. Her daughter had to learn to slay her own dragons. It was a lesson Bethany had to learn the hard way when Griff left her.

As Bethany watched Griff work, she realized coming here was probably going to be the second biggest mistake of her life.

The first was when she had married Griff.

AFTER GRIFF SECURED his truck on the ferry, he surveyed everything around him for any sign of trouble. He would continue to be on guard until he got Bethany and Ada to a secure location. So far, everything appeared clear.

The ferry was full today, with at least forty cars, as it often was in the summer. Tourists with their vehicles loaded down with kayaks, beach chairs, and surfboards waited for their dream vacations to begin on Lantern Beach.

Griff wished he was headed to the island with those same thoughts of relaxation and carefree days on his mind.

But that wasn't the case. Protecting Bethany and Ada was his only concern. Nothing else mattered anymore.

As Ada fussed in the backseat, Bethany turned to him. "Do you think we could step out of the truck? It's getting hot in here, and I see other people are standing near the railing looking at the water. It might be a nice distraction. Besides, Ada and I have been sitting in a car for hours."

The truth was that Griff would prefer they all stay in the truck. That he could tuck Bethany and

Ada away until danger passed. But he knew that with a three-year-old what was ideal was not always what happened.

"That's fine." Griff opened his door and carefully took Ada from her car seat.

If he had his way, he'd never let his little girl go. But, sometimes, in order to do what was best for a person, you had to do the hard things in life.

Like saying goodbye.

Griff's pulse pounded at his temples at the thought.

The decision was something Bethany would never understand, and for which Ada would probably never forgive him. But deep down in his heart, Griff knew that putting space between himself and his wife and daughter had been the right thing.

Despite that, trouble had found them anyway.

"Daddy." Ada's fingers splayed against his cheek as she stared up at him.

"How's my girl?" Griff murmured, his former Navy SEAL persona disappearing. He was putty in this girl's hands, undoubtably.

He was rewarded with a big toothy grin.

"I've missed you, Daddy."

"I've missed you, sweetheart."

He glanced beside him at Bethany. She was just

as beautiful as ever—maybe even more so. Her sand-colored hair hung halfway down her back in silky locks. Her brown eyes were big and intelligent. Her features were gentle, the kind a person could look at all day and never get tired of.

The first thing he'd fallen in love with when he'd met Bethany was her heart. She would give away everything she owned to help others. Her gentle voice spoke encouragement, and she always had a listening ear for anyone in need.

She was entirely too good for him. Griff had always known that. Yet he hadn't been able to resist when the woman of his dreams walked into his life.

He only wished things hadn't ended the way they did. But it was too late for regrets.

As Ada patted his cheek, Griff glanced over the railing. Water surrounded the boat, and the scent of the sea rose up around them, tempered by a balmy breeze.

"Let's go look at the water," he murmured. "How does that sound?"

Ada grinned and nodded. "Water!"

They wove between the cars until they reached the railing. Ada's face lit up as she pointed at the gentle waves of the Pamlico Sound.

"Ooh, pretty," she murmured.

"Isn't it, though?" Griff pointed toward a small island in the distance, one with a few trees and lots of marsh grass. "See that? It's called Seagull Island. A Native American princess was once banished to that island for falling in love with the wrong person."

"What happened?"

"She called to the dolphins, and they came to her. She held on to their fins, and they pulled her across the water and took her home. When her tribe saw what had happened, they knew she was special. She eventually became one of the first female chiefs in their tribe."

"Warrior Princess," Ada said.

Griff grinned. "That's right. Warrior Princess."

"You two are just like each other, you know." Bethany touched Ada's hair, an unreadable expression on her face.

"I beg to differ," Griff said. "Ada is not devastatingly handsome."

"Oh, stop." Bethany rolled her eyes and let out a puff of laughter. "You were always so full of yourself."

"You know you missed it." He winked.

This wasn't the time to joke or to give Bethany a hard time. But it came as naturally as breathing.

With his sunglasses still on, Griff glanced back, maintaining a lookout for any trouble. A figure on the other side of the ferry caught his eye. A man had been watching the three of them. He'd quickly looked away when Griff spotted him.

It might not be anything.

But it could be something.

Griff knew that was a risk he couldn't take. If there was any chance that man was trouble, he needed to know.

Bethany's face went still as she stared at him. "Why do you have that look?"

"What look?"

"That look that says you're back on the battlefield."

He handed Ada to her. Bethany could read him too well. "Listen, get back in the truck and lock the doors. Understand?"

Bethany's face went still. "You're scaring me, Griff."

"Just do it. Okay?" He didn't have time to convince her. If that guy was trouble, Griff had to act now if he wanted to protect his family.

Fear welled in Bethany's gaze. But she listened and wove back through the cars until she reached his truck. Griff watched as she climbed inside, put Ada on her lap, and locked the door.

Now he had to find the man who'd been watching them. Until Griff knew if this guy was connected with the earlier abduction attempt, the stranger would remain a suspect in Griff's mind. Anyone who put Bethany and their daughter in danger was officially Griff's enemy.

He dodged several vehicles, scooted past tourists, and nodded to a member of the crew until he reached the other side of the boat.

Griff spotted the man again. Tall. Dark hair. Scruffy beard.

The man slipped behind a car, walking toward the bow of the boat.

Was he trying to give Griff the slip? Maybe.

That wasn't going to slow Griff down.

"Hey!" Griff yelled, stepping toward him.

The man looked back. Froze.

In the next instant, the stranger took off in a run.

CHAPTER THREE

BETHANY SAT in the front seat of Griff's truck and held Ada close, lifting silent but fervent prayers. She'd heard Griff yell. Sensed an urgency about him.

But Griff was out of sight. The cabin at the center of the boat blocked her view, and she had no idea what was going on.

What had Griff seen that made him react like that? Was it the man who'd tried to snatch Ada? Had the guy somehow managed to follow them aboard the ferry?

Her heart beat faster.

"Love you, Mommy." Ada touched Bethany's feather-shaped earring.

Bethany smiled. "I love you too, darling."

Ada continued to play with Bethany's earrings, temporarily distracted.

Bethany's thoughts drifted again. She'd been so careful on the way here. Just like Griff taught her, she'd looked in her rearview mirror. She'd turned where turning wasn't necessary. All in order to lose anybody who might be following.

She wanted to believe she was overreacting to all of this. But there was no overreacting involved here. The situation made her feel like she'd been sucker punched.

She remembered hearing the police mention the Savages. Could the person behind Ada's attempted abduction really be a terrorist? It just didn't seem within the realm of possibility in her simple little life.

But when Bethany had married a SEAL, she'd opened her life up to all kinds of secrets that she had no knowledge about. How was this all connected? As soon as she had some alone time with Griff, she was going to ask him.

"I want Daddy," Ada announced.

Ada tried to stand, to get out of Bethany's grip, and to explore more of the truck. Maybe she wanted to catch a glimpse of her dad whom she loved so much.

"Not now," Bethany said. "He'll be back in a minute."

Bethany lifted more prayers. Faster prayers. More desperate prayers.

They were kind of her thing. Especially lately.

As she glanced around again, she sensed something shift.

Everybody on the ferry seemed to freeze.

Bethany wanted to see what was going on for herself, but she couldn't risk exposing her daughter to potential danger. The truck was the safest place for them to be ... she hoped.

Shouting sounded in the distance. More footsteps rushed across the metal grates of the deck. People darted back into their cars, sheltering their children as they moved.

Bethany waited, but she didn't hear anything except Ada cooing on her lap. No bullets whizzed through the air. No one ran toward her.

Bethany could hardly breathe. What if the man from the park appeared? What if he tried to take Ada again? If he had a gun, Bethany would be powerless to stop him and ...

Panic tried to claim her.

Bethany couldn't let that happen. Griff was here.

Despite his shortcomings, he would protect her with his life if it came down to it.

The ferry had slowed, Bethany realized.

She glanced around. They weren't at the dock. Land was still only a sliver in the distance.

What was happening?

Finally, Griff jogged toward her.

He looked fine. Thank goodness. Bethany's shoulders sagged with temporary relief.

She braced herself for whatever he had to say. Her gut told her it wouldn't be good.

GRIFF FELT the tension mounting in his muscles as he climbed inside his truck and slammed the door.

"Are you okay?" Bethany stared at him, the words rushing from her lips.

"I'm fine. I saw someone who fit the description of the man you told me about. He was watching us. When I went to talk to him, he ran."

She sucked in a breath and rubbed Ada's back. "Did you catch him? Where is he?"

Griff grimaced as he remembered how things had played out. "When he saw me coming and realized there was nowhere to go, he jumped into the water."

Bethany's eyes widened. "He jumped off the ferry? Why would he do that?"

"It was the easiest way to get away, I suppose." Griff may have done the same thing if he'd been cornered.

"Did anyone go in after him?"

Griff had been about to go into the water himself. But then he'd stopped. What if that had been the plan? For Griff to chase this man and leave Bethany and Ada exposed? What if the man was working with somebody else who waited for Griff to do that so he could move in?

Griff couldn't take that risk.

"A crewmember jumped in after him but couldn't find him," Griff said.

"He just disappeared?" Bethany's eyes widened with disbelief. "How is that possible? It's a long swim back to shore."

"But it's not impossible. I'm sure officials will send another crew to look for him."

Her hand washed over her face as shock captured her features. It was a lot for anyone to comprehend, especially when coupled with the fact that Ada was potentially at the center of everything. "I can't believe this."

"These guys can't be messed with. It's why I wanted you to come here."

"But in Lantern Beach, there's nowhere to escape. If these guys come after me, I'm stuck on this island."

"You'll be with me and the rest of the Blackout guys. We're going to catch them, and we're going to end this."

A frown tugged at her lips. "I hope you're right."

"Catch them, Daddy. Catch them. Warrior." Ada jabbed her finger into his chest.

He tried to smile, tried to set his daughter at ease. But this just might be his toughest mission yet. Mostly because of what was at stake—the people that meant more to him than anything else in the world.

CHAPTER FOUR

FOR THE REST of the trip to Lantern Beach, Bethany could hardly swallow because of the lump in her throat. What happened to that man? What if he survived in the water and came after her again? Even worse, what if Griff and his friends couldn't help? What if this was bigger than them?

She glanced at Ada as she sat in the backseat. Her daughter looked at a picture book, totally immersed and totally clueless about the danger circling them.

Not Bethany. Her head still spun, and her pulse pounded too quickly. This was all such a nightmare. She felt certain she would wake up any minute now and resume her normal life. But that wouldn't be happening.

Griff pulled his truck to a stop in front of a cottage surrounded by six colorful cabanas out back. Sand dunes ripe with seagrass promised that the ocean was close, and seagulls flying overhead begged anyone nearby to listen to their cry. In other circumstances, this would be perfect.

"This is where you'll be staying." Griff cut the engine and turned toward her.

"It's right on the beach," Bethany said, trying to look on the bright side. "I've always wanted to stay oceanfront."

Half his lip tugged up in a smile. "I thought you'd like it. I'll get your stuff in a minute, but I'll let the guys say hi first."

Bethany felt a quake of nerves as she climbed from the truck. She started to get Ada, but Griff beat her to it. The way he held his daughter in his arms made it look like he never wanted to let go.

Bethany's heart pounded as bittersweet feelings gripped her. Ada deserved to have her dad in her life. Bethany would never forgive Griff for not wanting to be a part of their daughter's future. It was one thing to hurt Bethany but an entirely different story to hurt her daughter.

With one arm holding Ada, Griff placed his other hand on Bethany's back as he led her upstairs to the cottage. Just feeling his touch sent a shiver through her.

Bethany wanted to grumble beneath her breath. The last thing she needed was to feel warm fuzzies when she was around the man who'd broken her heart and abandoned her.

On second thought, maybe that wasn't a warm fuzzy feeling. Maybe it was the scorching hot sting of betrayal.

All of that was forgotten when she reached the screened-in porch and the old crew greeted her. Griff's best buddies from his SEAL team. The ones Bethany had shared dinners with, whom she'd celebrated alongside, whom she'd mourned with. Those things bonded people for life.

Immediately, Dez Rodriguez swept Ada from Griff's arms and gave her a twirl. Dez, the charming troublemaker of the group. His picture had appeared in a magazine recently with popstar Bree Jordan, and Bethany wondered what their story was.

Maybe she would find out later.

Ada giggled, almost as if she remembered Dez. Was that possible? It had been nearly a year since her daughter had seen him.

Benjamin James was also there—Angel Eyes, as

the guys had called the youngest, newest member of their team.

Ty Chambers, who wasn't on Griff's team but who was a friend, stood near the door, a golden retriever wagging its tail beside him.

The guys had always made a big deal over Ada. They'd said that she would be the most guarded little girl on the East Coast, and, as Bethany watched them now, she didn't doubt it.

"Bethany," a soft voice said.

In the middle of all the testosterone, Elise Oliver appeared. Elise with her petite build, smattering of freckles, and glossy brown hair. Bethany had never been so glad to see another woman.

Her old friend pulled her into a hug. "It's so good to see you, Bethany."

"What are you doing here?" Bethany said, still touching Elise's arm. Of all the people she'd expected, Daniel Oliver's widow wasn't one of them.

"It's a long story, but I'm hanging out here for a while. I'm helping with the organization that Ty started called Hope House."

Colton Locke stepped onto the porch and gave Bethany a hug before wrapping an arm around Elise's shoulders. "It's good to see you, Bethany."

Bethany's lips parted. Elise and Colton? There

was definitely a story here. But now that Bethany saw the two of them together, she realized what a great couple they made.

She smiled when she saw the way Elise beamed. It was good to see her friend happy again. After Daniel had been killed during a training exercise, Bethany feared her friend would never find joy again. The two of them obviously had some catching up to do.

Almost as if this was a reunion instead of a bodyguard mission, they all went inside and shared a meal that Dez and Colton had prepared. It *was* dinnertime. It had been a long, long day.

Being with everyone felt like old times. Something about it made Bethany a little heartsick.

The way she thought her life would turn out, and the way it actually *had* turned out were two completely different things. There were times that Bethany desperately missed this part of her old life.

She sat back and listened to the guys rib each other. Watched Griff looking so happy, so much like he'd moved on. She observed Colton and Elise, both getting second chances at love.

Bethany . . . she'd merely been surviving. She wasn't complaining. She loved being a mother. But between work and taking care of Ada, the rest of her life was a blur.

She didn't often admit to people just how hard it had been when Griff left. But her heart hadn't been the same since. Maybe it never would be.

What she'd told Cindi was the truth—Bethany wasn't ready to date again. Nor did she have time to. In the back of her mind, maybe she'd hoped Griff felt the same way. That maybe he felt incomplete without her.

Looking at him now as he joked with Benjamin, it sure didn't seem that way.

As the sun began to set, Ada's eyes began to droop.

"Let me show you where you're staying tonight," Griff said. "I'll get you moved in so Ada can rest."

Bethany nodded, another tremble of nerves raking through her. "That would be great."

But she dreaded being alone with Griff again and began praying for a good dose of patience and a whole lot of forgiveness.

GRIFF OPENED the door to his cabana and let Bethany and Ada slip inside. He'd loaded his arms with luggage and set everything just inside the doorway.

"You guys can stay in here," he told them. "With me."

Bethany's eyes widened as she glanced around. The place was adorable—but small. There was a double bed, two chairs with a small table, a kitchenette, and a loft. She assumed that through one doorway was a bathroom and a closet through the other.

It was ... tight in here.

She glanced back at Griff, uncertain if she'd heard correctly. "With you?"

Griff's hands went to his hips and that stubborn look returned to his eyes. "I'm not letting you out of my sight."

"But there's just a double bed in here." She pointed to the tightly tucked bedspread. Griff had always loved for his space to be tidy and neat. Some things hadn't changed.

He shrugged, that cool look still in his eyes. "I have a cot. I'll sleep on it. No big deal."

Bethany gave him a look.

Griff shrugged again. "What? It's not like I've never seen you sleep before. I know you drool sometimes, but I think it's adorable."

If Bethany wasn't so mad at him, she might slap his chest. That would seem too much like flirting. She couldn't risk *that* miscommunication.

They were two adults. Certainly, they could handle this situation together. She was just grateful to have a place to stay.

"Fine," she said with a resigned sigh. "We'll stay in here."

"I promise I'll be good." Griff held up his hand in the Boy Scout pledge.

"And I promise that, if you're not, I will tap into all of those Navy SEAL skills that you taught me, and I will make you regret it." Bethany tried to sound tough and to make her boundaries clear.

But she knew Griff wouldn't be making any moves. If he'd wanted to do that, he would have stayed married.

Instead of seeming threatened, a smile played on Griff's lips. "Besides, you always talked about how fun it would be to have a tiny house."

"That was before I realized how big your ego was," she shot back, trying not to smirk.

Griff let out a long, low chuckle before shaking his head. "Good one."

They'd always had lively banter. It was one of the few things they were good at as a couple. No, that wasn't true. But it *was* how things felt most of the time. At least, they did in retrospect.

"Let's get you settled."

Bethany grabbed Ada's bag. But, as she reached inside to grab some lotion, her hand felt something unfamiliar.

She pulled the mystery object out and held up a knife with something resembling dried blood on the edge.

Her gaze met Griff's. "What is this doing in Ada's bag?"

CHAPTER FIVE

"WHO ELSE HAD access to this bag?" Griff lowered himself on the end of the bed. As Ada ran over to him and raised her arms, he lifted her into his embrace. He wished he never had to let her go—especially after seeing the knife that had been nestled between her water bottle and favorite stuffed animal.

He'd picked up the knife with a paper towel and placed it inside a plastic bag to preserve any evidence. He needed to take it to the police chief in town so she could examine it for fingerprints and DNA. But first he wanted more information.

Griff didn't like any of this. Whoever left the knife wanted to send a message—a message to let them know he was close. Near enough to touch them. And that he would be back, no doubt. Danger continued to accelerate, and the tension across his chest only grew.

"Ada was at daycare yesterday. I suppose anyone who works there could have gotten into the bag." Bethany shrugged, worry clouding her gaze. She offered a tight smile at Ada, as if she tried to put their daughter at ease.

"Anyone else?"

Bethany sat back in one of the chairs near the window and scrubbed a hand over her face. "I had it at the police station and at the park also. I . . . I don't know."

Griff bit down. More than anything, he wanted to reach out to her. To try to offer comfort. But he knew his touch wouldn't be welcome. He also knew it wouldn't be a good idea considering their history.

None of this was supposed to happen. When Griff left, trouble was supposed to leave with him. So why was someone targeting his family now?

"If you remember anything else, let me know," Griff said.

Bethany nodded. He already missed her bubbly retorts. The times when she tried to sound mean, but she couldn't. She didn't have it in her. Right now, she just looked frightened and overwhelmed—as she should.

"Listen," Griff started. "I need to go talk to the guys, tell them what's going on. We have to set up a plan to keep you safe, and we have no time to waste. When I get back, we'll talk? I'll let you know what I know."

"Okay. That will give me time to get Ada to sleep."

Griff stood, hesitant to leave, especially as Ada gripped him more tightly. Everything he wanted in the whole wide world was right here. But he had no choice but to hand Ada over to Bethany, especially if he wanted to find some answers.

He lingered one more minute. "I'll station a guy outside, okay? No one will get to you."

"Thank you." Bethany shoved a lock of hair behind her ear, but her eyes still looked glazed and her features too pale.

"I'll be back, baby girl," Griff murmured, kissing Ada's cheek.

His daughter grinned and leaned forward, her lips skimming Griff's nose. "Love you, Daddy."

His heart nearly broke right there as he remembered everything he'd lost—all for a job that sometimes felt meaningless.

He handed Ada to Bethany, took one last look at them, and then stepped toward the door. Above all, he had to keep these two safe, no matter the cost.

"SO A MEMBER of the Savages is behind this?" Dez rubbed his jaw, a contemplative expression on his face as he leaned back in his chair.

He, Griff, and Colton had gathered in Colton's cabana. The space was tight but worked for what they needed. Plus, Griff was close to Bethany and Ada. His place was next door, less than fifteen feet away.

Benjamin had volunteered to sit outside Griff's cabana and keep an eye on Bethany and Ada until Griff could get back. But Griff was anxious to put his eyes on them again.

"The police identified the license plate of a car that fled the scene as belonging to someone associated with the terrorist group." Griff leaned forward, elbows perched on his legs as he shared what he knew. "I put in a call to see if they'd give me a name, but I haven't heard back yet."

"Why would a member of the Savages want

Ada?" Colton shook his head. "It doesn't make sense."

That question was all Griff had been able to think about since Bethany told him what happened at the park.

"There's only one reason I can think of—leverage." Nausea churned in Griff's stomach as he said the words. He didn't want to believe they were true, but he'd regret not considering the option. Being in denial of the truth would only get them killed.

"You think they're targeting Ada so they can use her as leverage?" Colton's jaw flexed, but his voice made it clear he didn't disagree.

"Think about it." Griff straightened. "Out of all of us, I'm the only one who has a child. If you want to target anyone, a child is the most vulnerable."

Anger burned through his veins at the thought. Anyone who preyed on the innocent, the helpless... they were despicable. If anyone ever hurt Ada, Griff would make sure they paid. There were some boundaries that shouldn't be crossed.

"But leverage for what?" Dez rubbed the rosary tattoo on his arm, almost as if he was lifting up silent prayers. "Jason is behind bars. We're out of their hair, right?"

A few months ago, the Blackout team had discovered a traitor at the command their SEAL team had been based out of. This man, Jason Perkins, had been planted by the Savages to feed information to the group.

His actions had resulted in Daniel Oliver being killed. When Elise had discovered a secret box of information her husband had left behind, she'd become a target. The Savages were desperate to get that information back.

Though Jason was behind bars, Griff and his colleagues still suspected there was an enemy working within the confines of their old command.

"I've always wondered if we just skimmed the surface when Jason was arrested." A shadow hooded Colton's gaze as he said the words. "I didn't want to say anything. I was hoping I was reading too much into things."

Griff frowned. "Me too."

"The thought crossed my mind also." Dez glanced at all of them, his expression matching theirs. "So what do we do now?"

"The people behind this . . . they're going to come back. I have no doubt that they're not done yet." Griff explained what had happened on the ferry. Last he'd heard, the body of the man who'd jumped overboard had not been found. It probably wouldn't be. The man had most likely managed to escape. "They know where we are."

"Then we'll need to hunker down and protect Bethany and Ada here," Colton said.

"They're safer with us in Lantern Beach than they are anywhere else," Dez agreed.

Griff didn't argue. Sometimes running wasn't the solution and hiding wasn't an option. The best thing a person could do was prepare and execute a plan.

"Bethany and Ada shouldn't go anywhere without one of us," Colton said. "Two of us is even better."

"I agree," Griff said. "In the meantime, I'll follow up with Anderson Bryant and see if he's heard anything yet."

Griff had put out some feelers with one of his friends who was still a SEAL. He wanted to know what the scuttlebutt was around the Savages right now. Anderson seemed like a good source to get that information from, and Griff knew he could trust the man.

They ended the meeting and stood, ready to retire back to their cabanas for the evening. Before Griff left, Colton called to him.

Based on the look on his leader's face, Griff wasn't going to like this conversation.

Colton lowered his voice. "You going to be okay having Bethany and Ada here? I know the split has been hard on you."

Griff hesitated a moment. He wanted to deny his friend's words, but he knew it would do no good. His friends knew him. They'd been there for him throughout everything.

But Griff *could* handle this. There was no way he wasn't going to protect Bethany and Ada—even if being around them was like torture for his heart and soul.

Finally, he nodded. "Yeah, of course. I'll be fine."

The gleam in Colton's eyes clearly stated he didn't believe him. But his friend didn't call him out. Not yet, at least.

"If you're not, let me know," Colton said. "Okay?"

Griff nodded again. "Sure."

Now it was time for Griff to get back to his cabana and attempt to have a conversation with Bethany.

He had a lot to tell her. He only hoped she received the information well.

Griff dismissed Benjamin from guard duty, stood in front of his cabana door, and braced himself for his upcoming conversation.

Bethany was the sweetest girl in the entire world.

But Griff seemed to bring out a fire in her. He'd be remiss if he didn't admit that he loved seeing the sparks ignite in her eyes.

Maybe he even instigated the reaction sometimes.

But he couldn't stand to see her truly mad at him. It was his weakness.

Bethany was the good girl. The preacher's daughter. A sweetheart to everyone she met.

Her family had been afraid Griff would corrupt her. After all, he was from a dysfunctional household. His parents were divorced. His mom was an alcoholic, and his dad had been absent. Griff had nearly been kicked out of high school after getting in with the party crowd.

Joining the Navy had saved Griff from going down a very bad path.

But meeting Bethany had changed him into a better man. At least, it had until Daniel died. His leader's death had flipped his world upside down.

After another moment of hesitation, Griff pushed the door to his cabana open, prepared for a verbal lashing—one that he deserved.

Instead, Bethany was curled up in his bed asleep with Ada snoozing beside her. The two of them looked so peaceful and cozy as they snuggled next to each other.

Emotion clogged his throat.

Had there ever been a more beautiful sight?

He didn't think so.

Seeing them reminded Griff of everything he'd given up, and a pang echoed in his heart. He'd missed them so much.

These two were never supposed to wander back into his life like this.

Yet here they were.

He shook his head.

None of that mattered. The only thing Griff needed to focus on was keeping them safe. And that's exactly what he planned on doing.

With that thought in mind, he found a spare blanket in the closet and draped it over them. Then he slipped onto his cot. He would attempt to get some sleep tonight.

But, between the danger and Bethany and Ada being here, he knew it would be nearly impossible.

CHAPTER SIX

CASSIDY CHAMBERS WAS quiet as she walked into her house that evening. It had been a long day at work, and she couldn't wait to kick back and relax for a few minutes.

The last session of Hope House had ended yesterday, so she and Ty had the house to themselves tonight. The only other person staying here right now was the house manager Ty had recently hired, but CJ had taken a couple days off.

All was quiet and dark in the house as Cassidy crept down the hallway and softly opened the door to their bedroom. Ty sat at a small desk in the corner, staring at the computer screen when she walked in. She leaned in from behind him and kissed his cheek.

"Hey, honey." Ty turned away from the computer long enough to reach up and peck her cheek. "How are you doing?"

"It's been a day. Based on how tense you look, it's been a day for you also." She placed her gun in the safe below her nightstand. "What's going on?"

Ty turned around in the chair to face her, and Cassidy saw the exhaustion on his face. "You heard about the jumper on the ferry?"

"Of course." She sat on the edge of the bed. "It was all the talk for the day. At least, it was all the talk for part of the day. That's another story."

"Yeah, well that guy may have tried to abduct Griff's daughter..."

Cassidy's eyes widened. "Why didn't I hear about this? There were no police reports."

"It didn't happen here. It happened in Virginia Beach. Bethany and Ada came here to get away. Griff met them on Hatteras, but he saw someone suspicious on the ferry ride over. When he tried to confront him, the man jumped in the water."

Cassidy ran a hand over her face. "Wow. That was Griff who reported it? I sent Officer Banks over to take a statement from the crew. Nothing about the kidnapping attempt was mentioned."

"Griff's trying to keep Bethany's presence here on

the down low," Ty said. "We were all surprised when we heard what happened."

"Where are Bethany and Ada now?"

"They're staying in the cabana with Griff."

Cassidy raised her eyebrows. "I thought the two of them had a pretty contentious relationship."

"I don't know if I would say contentious. You know how Griff is. On a good day, he's aggravating and contrary. And Bethany doesn't take it. She gives it right back to him. But when their daughter is around, both of them seem to forget all their differences and become different people."

"I guess children can do that to you. Hopefully, they won't have any more trouble now that they're here."

"That's something I wanted to talk to you about." Ty pulled an object from his drawer. "This was found in Ada's bag. Griff asked me to give it to you."

He held up a bag containing a knife with dried blood on its serrated edges.

Cassidy's eyes widened as she took the bag from him and examined the knife. "They have no idea where this came from?"

"No idea. Ada goes to daycare, so someone could have potentially put it in her bag there. They were also at the park when Ada was nearly abducted, and apparently the bag was sitting on a bench for a while unattended. Basically, Bethany doesn't know."

Cassidy continued to stare at the knife. "I'm assuming it was left there as a threat."

"That's my guess also."

"First thing in the morning, I'll run this for prints and see if we can pick up anything from the blood."

"Thanks."

"And whatever you guys need to keep this little girl safe, just let me know. A child predator has no place on this island." As the words left her lips, Cassidy felt sick to her stomach. Whoever had tried to grab Ada had been brazen. What else did this person have planned?

Ty leaned back and closed his eyes a moment. "I guess you and your guys have a lot on your hands with the hotel situation. I hardly heard from you today, which usually means you're busy."

Cassidy frowned as a replay of her day buzzed through her mind. "You can say that again. Ever since the measure to stop the hotel from being built was shot down by the county and the developer decided to go ahead with the project, people have been all up in arms again."

Islanders were opposed to a new six-story hotel that had just been approved to be built on the island.

It would be the first establishment in Lantern Beach that wasn't locally owned. The infrastructure here wasn't ready for that kind of growth. That's what those opposed said. Those in favor looked forward to the extra money the additional tourists would bring.

The whole issue had been a hot topic since the site was proposed several months ago.

"Have they made any progress yet?" Ty asked.

"They began dredging."

Ty's eyes widened. "Filling in the marsh?"

Cassidy frowned and nodded. "Yep."

"I can't believe the environmentalists haven't stepped in."

"Me too. It's a shame to see the marsh being destroyed. We need that area to filter the water in the bay and keep wildlife alive. But money wins. At least, that's all too often what happens."

"I wish I could argue that fact," Ty said. "But I can't."

"The project manager is about as unfriendly as they come. They've also started digging a big hole. I'm assuming that's where the septic system and pipes and foundation for the hotel will be." She shrugged. "I'm not really sure. But we've gotten so many calls from the developer about this that I've basically assigned Officer Dillinger to stay at the hotel property for his shift each day. Too many people are going to the site and trying to protest. I don't want anyone to get hurt."

"I can't believe the hotel is being built. It just blows my mind."

"I know. Me too."

Ty stood and ran a hand over his face. "I guess that's enough working for me tonight."

"What have you been doing on that computer?"

"We believe that this attempted kidnapping had something to do with the Savages. Even though the last incident with Jason Perkins was reported to the command, I haven't heard anything about it since then. I was checking to see if any news articles have come out."

"And have they?"

"Not that I can find."

"Maybe some sleep would do you good."

"Some sleep sounds like just what the doctor ordered." But instead of reaching for his pajamas, Ty reached for Cassidy and pulled her into a long, lingering kiss.

CHAPTER SEVEN

BETHANY JOLTED UPRIGHT IN BED, a cold sweat covering her skin.

She glanced around. Saw the cabana. Saw Ada snoozing beside her. Spotted the blue sky through a skylight and the cheerful sunlight flooding into the room.

She really was here. In Lantern Beach. With Griff.

None of that had been a nightmare.

Her little girl had almost been kidnapped.

And it wasn't over yet.

Bethany squeezed her eyes shut. She'd had a brief moment of hoping—believing—it was all just a bad dream.

But it wasn't.

She opened her eyes again and scanned everything around her one more time, trying to get her bearings. Ada still slept soundly, cuddled up next to her in bed. Their bags were still near the door. Bethany had fallen asleep before she could unpack.

Her gaze stopped across the room to where Griff slept on a cot.

He seemed to sense her eyes on him and pushed himself up. His hair fell into his face, and his eyes were hazy with sleep. For a moment, Bethany was whisked back in time. Whisked back to when the two of them had been happily married. To the lazy mornings they'd spent together in bed.

Those times had been so happy, so full of hope. Now they were all a bittersweet memory of what could have been . . . if Griff hadn't turned his back on them.

As the blanket fell around his waist, Bethany's mouth dropped open.

"Where's your shirt?" Bethany whispered as loudly as she could without waking Ada.

Griff glanced down and shrugged, as laid-back as ever. "I never sleep with a shirt. You know that."

"But shouldn't you sleep with a shirt on when we're here?" Seriously, they were on the same page, right?

Maybe not.

"I didn't think it was a big deal." He shrugged.

"Well, it is. Boundaries and everything."

"Okay, okay. I get it. I just didn't think much of it."

"Of course you didn't."

A gleam appeared in his gaze. "I mean, we have made a baby together. It's not like you've never seen my chest before."

Bethany's cheeks flushed, and she narrowed her eyes. "I'm well aware. But that was different."

"Touché." He grabbed a T-shirt from beside him and pulled it on. "Better?"

Bethany swallowed hard. "Yes. Thank you."

She looked away. Was it the fact that Griff didn't have a shirt on that bothered her? Or the fact that he looked so good without a shirt on? His finely sculpted chest was a sight to behold.

Which was exactly why she didn't want to admire it. All the good looks in the world meant nothing without a person of character embodying them.

"After we get ready, we can have breakfast in the cottage," Griff said. "Are you okay with that?"

Bethany nodded and pulled her hair back into a ponytail. Getting out of this small cabin she shared with Griff sounded great.

Besides, she desperately wanted updates, something that pointed at an end to this nightmare. If she had to walk through the fire to get there, she would. "Sure. We do have a lot to talk about."

"You were sleeping when I got back last night."

"I didn't think I would be able to sleep. I guess I was wrong." She'd been out cold.

"After your burst of adrenaline, you crashed. Totally normal."

Griff sounded like he really cared—though Bethany was certain he didn't. In fact, something about this whole conversation rubbed her the wrong way. It felt too normal when nothing was normal.

Instantly, her guard went back up. She had to be more careful. She needed to protect herself.

Bethany stood and grabbed her bag. "I guess I need to get ready. Somewhere private."

Griff nodded toward the door. "How about if I wait on the porch?"

"Perfect."

Some space from the man was exactly what Bethany needed. But the fact that they were on the same island meant she wouldn't be getting nearly enough any time soon.

GRIFF COULDN'T HELP but marvel at Bethany and Ada during breakfast. He did his best not to stare, not to show how thrilled he was to see them again. Instead, he tried to concentrate on the French toast and sausage that Dez had awoken early to make.

His colleagues were busy amusing Ada by making faces and pretending to sneak her food. Her giggles filled the room and made everything in the world feel right, if only for a minute.

Griff's gaze stopped on Bethany again. She was so good with Ada.

A memory of the first time he'd seen her filled his mind. Griff had been in the military for four years, and Daniel had invited him to church. Griff had been uncomfortable from the moment he'd stepped inside, but he had been determined to go once, get it over with, and never go back again.

Then he'd seen Bethany singing in the choir, and he'd been enamored.

He'd found himself back at church week after week after seeing her for the first time. Eventually, he'd even managed to show up to Bethany's Sunday school class. They'd been in the same prayer circle at the end. When Griff had mentioned he was in the military and was thinking about trying out for SEAL training, Bethany's eyes had met his and she'd smiled.

"You should go for it," she'd told him.

He was already in love, and the two of them had never even been on a date. But Griff was determined to ask her out. Only, every time he started, he faltered. One day, Bethany had asked him to help with a building project in a local low-income neighborhood. While there, they'd talked. Flirted. Connected.

Bethany seemed so out of his league. Despite that, Griff had finally managed to ask if she wanted to have dinner together the next day. She'd said yes. When Griff had admitted that he was nervous, Bethany had asked why. He'd told her it was because she seemed too perfect, especially compared to him.

She laughed. Told him about her shortcomings. About how she held grudges, especially when people hurt her family. How she loved validation. How she had a touch of a rebellious spirit at times.

Those things only made her seem more perfect.

But Griff remembered those words now. *I hold grudges, especially when people hurt my family.*

Bethany had to have the ultimate grudge against him now. Griff would never forget her expression when he'd told her he was leaving. Her eyes had been orbs of hurt, so full of pain that the image haunted Griff's sleep at night. He wasn't even sure he could ever forgive himself.

Maybe it was better that she kept her walls up. They needed to keep their distance.

As they finished eating, Dez and Ty left to go down to the ferry. They'd taken Kujo, Ty's dog, with them. The man who'd jumped yesterday had left his car onboard, and Cassidy had given them permission to look at it.

That left Benjamin, Griff, and Colton here at the cottage, along with Elise. Colton had some administrative work to do for Blackout and would be working in his cabana for a while.

Griff's eyes met Bethany's. "You want to take a walk and talk?"

"I'll watch Ada," Elise called. She was already sitting on the floor with the girl, drawing pictures on a pad of paper.

Bethany hesitated a moment before rising. "If you're sure, then okay. Let's go."

Griff prayed he would find the right words.

Because he was about to drop a bombshell on her.

CHAPTER EIGHT

AS GRIFF and Bethany stepped from Ty's cottage, he noticed the frown on Bethany's face. She was worried about leaving their daughter—like any mother would be in a situation like this.

"Ada will be fine," he assured her. "Elise loves kids, and Benjamin is stationed outside to keep an eye on everything."

"I know." Bethany shoved her hands into the pockets of her gray sweatshirt. "I trust both of them. It's just so hard to be away from Ada with all of this happening."

"I figured we could walk down to the beach and get some fresh air. Thought it might do you some good." Griff had known Bethany would love it. She'd always been a sucker for the beach.

"It does sound nice, especially with the weather like it is today. Plus, I don't want Ada overhearing too much. I know she's only three, and she can't possibly understand the implications of all that's happened. But the girl's got good intuition. She can sense when something is wrong."

They climbed down the stairs at the cottage, crossed over the dune, and their feet hit the sand on the other side. The ocean was beautiful today, almost a turquoise color, and the waves were gentle and rolling.

He glanced at Bethany and saw her eyes light up. Delight filled him. He'd always thought there was something healing about saltwater. He hoped being here might help Bethany also.

They continued to stroll along the shore together, their feet gently sinking into the sand and leaving two sets of impressions behind them.

"So, did I hear that Dez is dating popstar Bree Jordan?" Bethany started.

"You did. They met during her concert here in Lantern Beach."

"The one where the shooting occurred?"

Griff nodded. "Unfortunately, yes. But, despite the way they met, the two of them seem really happy together. She'll be back in a couple weeks to do another concert here. I know Dez is looking forward to seeing her."

"I never thought I'd see Dez in a serious relationship."

"Yeah, none of us did. But I guess when you meet the one, you just know." Griff's grin faded as his words sent a cold, stark reminder through his heart of what he'd lost. But he couldn't think like that. Not now, especially.

Right now, he needed to remain focused on keeping Bethany and Ada safe.

A few minutes of silence passed as they paced down the shoreline. Griff gave Bethany the time to sort her thoughts.

Finally, she cleared her throat and glanced at him. "Did you hear yet if they found the man who jumped off the ferry?"

"I checked in this morning, and they hadn't found his body yet. My guess is that this man somehow managed to get away and avoid being captured."

Bethany's lip drew into a thin line. "Whoever is behind this, he knows what he's doing, doesn't he? This isn't some amateur with no experience. Instead, these guys are thorough."

Griff frowned. "You could say that."

"Do you really think the Savages are responsible?"

"That's what I wanted to talk to you about." Griff sucked in a deep breath, knowing there were things he needed to say that he had no desire to say. It was better, however, just to rip the bandage off than to keep delaying the inevitable. "The guys and I . . . some of our last missions involved the Savages. We believe that one of them may be targeting us now."

Bethany froze on the sand and turned to him, her lips parting with surprise. "So you think Ada is a target because of that?"

Hearing the words leave Bethany's lips caused a grueling ache to rip through his heart. "I'm sorry, Bethany. It wasn't supposed to be this way."

She stared at him a moment as if processing the revelation and then she shook her head in disbelief. "How long have you known that Ada might be a target?"

"If I had any clue that these guys might take things to this extreme, believe me, I would have let you know about it. But I assumed it was just my former SEAL team in the crosshairs."

"Griff, you've got to tell me what's going on. I deserve to know that much."

More than anything, he wished he could spill the

truth to her, that he could tell her everything. But certain information was classified, and he was sworn to secrecy on it.

"You know I wish I could tell you more..."

She crossed her arms. "Then tell me what you do know, what you're allowed to say."

Griff ran a hand over his face and stared out over the water for a moment.

How much could he say? If the roles were reversed, he'd want all the facts.

He had to make a decision—a choice he could live with.

"LET'S SIT," Griff said.

Bethany didn't want to sit, but she did it anyway. If Griff's explanation had the implication she thought it would, this conversation was going to be a doozy. Maybe her legs wouldn't hold her up.

Bethany listened as Griff explained the situation to her—every grueling detail. She was thankful for the warm sunshine on her shoulders. It brought her a small measure of comfort. She would take whatever she could get in this gut-wrenching situation.

"So you're telling me that the Savages have a

personal vendetta against each of you and there could be someone who's been planted inside your former command who's feeding this group information?" Bethany repeated it out loud to make sure she understood.

Griff's gaze locked on hers. He meant business. His normal playfulness was gone. "This is all highly classified information that I'm giving you. I shouldn't even be sharing this much. But when I consider what's on the line, I think you deserve to know."

He was taking a risk, and Bethany appreciated that. Throughout their married life, she hadn't known where he was most of the time, just that he was answering the call of duty. But now her daughter was at risk, and that protocol meant nothing to her.

"So what have these guys done so far?" Did Bethany really want to know? Part of her said no. But she had to know the truth, had to know what she was up against.

Griff stared off into the distance a moment. "They went after Elise, for starters. Daniel had been talking to a CIA agent who suspected there was an insider within the command. They were both trying to track down who this person was when the CIA agent was killed."

"And then Daniel was killed during that training exercise, right?" She tried to put the pieces together, though she hated the picture that formed.

Griff's face turned to stone. There was obviously something he was not saying . . . Bethany waited for him to gather his thoughts.

He let out a long breath. "That training exercise was actually a black ops mission. Daniel, Colton, Dez, Benjamin, and I were all a part of it. We believe this traitor sold us out, and that the Savages knew we were coming. We were ambushed, and that's why Daniel died."

"No . . ."

Bethany gasped as the images played out in her mind. She'd had no idea. She'd only known that Daniel's death had been a turning point in her relationship with Griff. She'd assumed Griff suffered some kind of PTSD afterward. She knew when Griff left her, it had something to do with that time in his life. But she'd never expected this.

"I wish it wasn't true, but it is. We caught the mole. He was a member of the commander's entourage—one of his drivers, to be precise. He was in the perfect position to overhear private conversations. He then shared that information with the Savages."

Bethany rubbed her temples, still trying to make sense of things. "But if this guy is now behind bars, why are we still in danger?"

Griff found a broken shell in the sand beneath him and tossed it into the water. "That's what we are trying to figure out. Another member of the command, the commander's chief of staff Brian Starks, came to Lantern Beach about two months ago to tell us he suspected there was still a traitor in our midst. As he was leaving the island, he was run off the road, and he's still in a coma."

"That's awful... but I don't understand. Why are they targeting Blackout? You guys aren't Navy SEALs anymore, so why do they feel threatened by you?"

He pushed his sunglasses higher. "Because we started asking too many questions. Someone had to do it. Nobody else was stepping up. Maybe because nobody else knows."

"So if they eliminate all of you, then their secret is safe and they can continue on with their plans." Bethany's stomach clenched as she said the words. It all seemed surreal, like something that would happen in a movie, not in real life. But Griff wouldn't make something like this up, especially not if Ada was affected.

"Exactly," Griff said. "I just had no idea that they might target you and Ada in order to get to me."

Despite the sunshine, a shiver raked over Bethany. She pulled her knees closer to her chest and stared at the water. "I don't like this, Griff."

"Believe me, neither do I."

"What are we going to do?"

"We are still going to try to find answers. And, in the meantime, we're going to keep you safe."

It sounded so easy when he said it that way. But nothing about this was going to be easy. Terrorists were after them, for goodness sake.

"That seems almost like an impossible task. These guys—I assume there's more than one—went after Ada in the park. They somehow still managed to follow me here, even though I saw no one behind me during the drive. What will they do next?" Bethany watched Griff, waiting to see his reaction.

A frown twitched at his lips. "That's what we are all wondering."

She almost wished that Griff had denied her statement. That he would say all the scary stuff was done and over with. But that wasn't the case.

Bethany had always appreciated that Griff was forthright with his opinions—the good, the bad, and the ugly of them.

Just as the thought entered her mind, something in the distance caught her eye. She pointed to the sky. "Griff..."

Griff looked toward the cottage. Something hovered near the roof. It didn't move like a bird, so what could it be?

"That's a..." Griff shook his head, as if he didn't believe his eyes. "It's a drone. Come on."

The next instant, he grabbed her hand, and they took off running toward the cottage.

CHAPTER NINE

GRIFF'S MUSCLES burned as he sprinted through the sand toward the cottage. He didn't know what was going on, but he didn't like any of the conclusions that came to mind.

Thankfully, Bethany kept pace beside him. She'd always been a runner, and he was exceedingly grateful for that right now. His gut told him they had no time to waste.

As they reached the dune near Ty's cottage, he saw someone sprawled in the sand.

Benjamin.

Griff darted toward his friend and knelt beside him, quickly checking for wounds. He saw nothing.

"Benjamin?" Griff rushed. "What happened?"

The man's eyes fluttered open. He moaned

before rubbing his head. "I saw a drone. I went to check it out, and someone must have hit me over the head. I blacked out."

Griff's pulse quickened. "Where is Ada?"

Benjamin shook his head and pulled himself to his feet. He staggered, still unsteady. "I . . . I don't know. Go. I'll be fine."

Griff and Bethany darted toward the cottage. But it was too late.

A man in a black mask stood beneath the house, holding Elise and Ada hostage as he backed toward the lane in the distance. As Elise held Ada, the man shoved a gun to the woman's head. His other arm wrapped around both his hostages.

Tears streamed down Elise's face as she looked back at them. Her eyes communicated plenty. That she was sorry. Scared. Unsure.

And Ada . . . her eyes were wide and confused.

"Stay back or I'll shoot!" The man continued to back away with his hostages.

Griff paused where he was, not wanting to take any chances. "Let them go."

Bethany and Benjamin also froze behind him.

"It's too late for that," the man said. "If you know what's best, you'll step back."

Griff didn't move. "That's not going to happen."

"Please, let them go." Bethany's voice quivered, her gaze on their daughter. "Ada is just a little girl. She's not a part of this."

The man let out a little chuckle and backed up even more. "This is bigger than any of you know. If you had just left it alone, it wouldn't have come down to this."

Griff had to do something. But he couldn't put Ada or Elise at risk. Tension pulled inside him.

The man inched closer to the lane. Exactly what was he planning? Griff didn't see any cars waiting for him.

Something didn't make sense. How did the man think he was going to get away?

At once, the man let out a yelp. His arm loosened enough for Ada to scramble to the ground.

She'd bit him, hadn't she? Griff hid his smile.

That's my girl...

She rushed over to her mother's outstretched arms, and Bethany pulled her daughter into a tight embrace.

"Get her out of here," Griff said. "Benjamin—go with her."

Bethany hesitated only a moment before she ran back toward the cottage. Benjamin followed close behind her.

Now it was just Griff and this man with Elise.

From the corner of his eye, Griff saw some movement. Colton had stepped from his cabana.

The good news was that the man didn't appear to notice Colton. Griff didn't think so, at least.

They had to think of a way to get Elise away from this man. There couldn't be any more casualties. There had already been too many.

BETHANY HELD Ada in her arms and rocked her back and forth as she sat on the couch. Benjamin had led them back into the cottage and checked out the rest of the place. Everything appeared safe.

But nowhere was safe. Not really.

Life was driving home that reality again and again.

What was going on outside? Was Griff okay? How about Elise?

Bethany pressed her eyes shut and began whispering silent prayers. This nightmare didn't even seem real. How could she be a normal associate editor one day and going through this the next? It didn't seem right.

She pulled Ada closer and continued to rock her

in her arms. But Ada seemed okay. Bethany was the one who needed comforting right now.

Warrior Princess.

Maybe Griff had it right when he called Ada that. The girl could be fearless at times. The fact that Ada had bitten her attacker's arm may have ended up saving her life.

Bethany couldn't stop the tears from streaming down her cheeks. She'd been so certain she was going to lose her daughter. So certain that man was going to take Ada and that Bethany would never see her again.

Thank goodness, that wasn't the case.

Benjamin stood near the window, still rubbing his head. That man must have hit him hard if it had knocked him out. Certainly, it had bruised his ego as well. Most SEALs she'd met didn't take well to anything they perceived as weakness.

"What's going on down there?" she asked Benjamin.

"I can't see anything. I'm not sure." Benjamin turned toward her, his expressive eyes orbs of regret and sorrow. "I'm sorry, Bethany. I'm not sure how that man snuck up on me like he did."

"I know you were doing everything you could to protect Ada and Elise."

"It was just that I saw that drone and . . . it was the perfect distraction, I suppose."

"I can see why it would be. These guys . . . aren't to be messed with, are they?"

"No, they are not. They keep getting scarier with each incident."

Bethany shivered. To hear a former Navy SEAL say that, she knew it must be serious. It wasn't that SEALs weren't afraid of things. But if they admitted that they were? Then you knew you had a reason to be concerned.

Bethany heard a shout outside, followed by gunfire.

She held her breath as her eyes met Benjamin's.

She had no idea what was going on, but she knew it couldn't be good.

Dear Lord, please be with them.

CHAPTER TEN

GRIFF WATCHED as the man continued to back up with Elise.

At once, the man's gaze shifted. He spotted Colton, and his actions became more frantic, his steps quicker.

Whatever happened, they couldn't let this guy get away with Elise. Griff felt certain there would be no happy ending if they did.

"Let her go," Colton called. "She has nothing to do with this."

"None of you have anything to do with this," the man called. "You should have stayed out of it. Now you have to pay the price."

"You don't want to do this . . ." Griff said. "You'll regret it. Believe me."

"But I do want to. Now, put your guns on the ground before I pull the trigger. I mean it." Elise let out a cry, as if the man had hurt her.

Colton and Griff glanced at each other before nodding and doing as the man said. They had little choice.

"Kick them toward me," the man continued.

Griff used his foot to push his gun out of reach. Colton did the same.

Colton stepped closer, his arms in the air. "Let her go. You can take me instead."

"No!" Elise yelled. "Colton . . ."

Colton didn't seem to hear. "She's not the one you want."

"Her husband was your leader. We had to take him out. We need to take her out also."

Anger shot through Griff at the way the man casually mentioned Daniel's death. The world had lost a great man that day—and the act of violence had been senseless.

"You're not going to get away with this, you have to know that," Griff growled.

The man was arrogant if he thought he was smarter than they were. As SEALs, they'd been trained to handle almost any situation that was thrown at them. This was no exception. They might falter at times, but they always won in the end.

"You might be surprised." The man's smirk came through loud and clear, even though they couldn't see his face.

"Don't do this." Colton's voice cracked. He was worried—and rightfully so.

The man reached the lane. Griff's gaze searched the area beyond it. He still saw no vehicles.

Certainly the man wasn't thinking about making a run for it. He had to understand they would catch him.

The bad feeling in Griff's gut continued to grow.

There was a chance this wouldn't end well. He couldn't let that happen. No more innocent lives could be lost.

"If you come any closer, I'll shoot her," the man yelled. "Don't test me."

Griff and Colton both stopped where they were.

Elise let out a cry again. "Colton..."

Griff's heart panged in his ears as he heard the desperation in her voice. If that was Bethany... Griff would be beside himself.

"I love you, Colton," she muttered.

"I love you too, Elise." Colton's voice sounded strained and throaty with emotion.

Elise was preparing for a goodbye, wasn't she? Pressure mounted inside Griff.

It couldn't end this way.

"Say your farewells!" The man raised the gun to Elise's temple.

Was this why there was no getaway vehicle? Because the man didn't plan on getting away?

Griff's blood went ice cold.

"No!" Colton shouted.

Griff braced himself as time seemed to turn to gel.

The next instant, he heard a muffled gunshot.

An ache began to spread through his chest.

And then . . . the masked man fell to the ground.

Elise nearly toppled there too, but Colton rushed forward and caught her. Gathered her in his arms. Kicked the man's gun out of the way.

What had just happened?

Griff looked down the lane and saw someone step from the marsh grass with a gun in hand.

CJ Compton.

Ty's newest hire—the house manager. The guys had been taking turns doing cooking and cleaning, but CJ was helping with the menial tasks that were important to day-to-day operations.

The woman was a pistol. She was only five feet

tall, with shiny brown hair often pulled back in a ponytail and a quick wit. She loved to wear Converse sneakers, and she could hang with the guys, matching wit for wit. Before coming to Lantern Beach, she'd worked as a bounty hunter.

She lowered her gun and nodded at them.

Griff rushed toward the man and checked for a pulse.

There was none.

Though Griff would have liked to get some information from the man, he knew that CJ had no choice. If she hadn't shot him when she did, Elise might be dead right now.

Griff stared at the man's still figure a moment before jerking his mask off.

A stranger's face stared back at him.

Surprising disappointment pressed on him. He wanted logic. He wanted for things to make sense. But they didn't. He had no idea who this man was.

Which meant they had no more answers than they did before.

"Look what I have," CJ called.

Griff looked up as she walked toward him. She reached into the marsh and held up something, displaying it like a hunter might display a duck during open season.

It was the drone.

"How did you get that?" Griff asked.

"I saw it hovering over the house and figured something was up," CJ said. "I parked at the end of the lane and crept this way. I knew it was trouble, so I shot it."

"Color me impressed," Griff muttered.

"I didn't hear any gunfire." Colton pulled Elise closer, looking like he never wanted to let go.

"I have a silencer." She held up her gun, looking totally at ease with the weapon.

"You must have been quite the bounty hunter." Griff liked this lady more and more all the time. Why in the world had she applied to work in the kitchen instead of the field?

She shrugged. "I like to think so."

"Either way, you saved my life," Elise said. "Thank you."

"Thank the person who sent me this text." CJ held up her phone.

"What text?" Colton's eyebrows shoved together in confusion.

CJ placed the drone on the ground and handed him her phone. "I didn't recognize the number."

"We need your help at Ty's place. Come now.

Come quietly," Colton read out loud. He glanced at Griff. "Did you send this?"

He shook his head. "Nope. Someone knocked Benjamin out. I doubt it was him."

"Dez and Ty aren't here right now," Elise said. "Who could have sent it?"

"I have no idea." Colton's jaw flexed. "It sounds like someone was watching out for us, though."

Whoever that person was may have saved Elise's life. So why did Griff still feel tense? "I should get inside to check on Bethany and Ada."

"I'll call the police," Colton said. But, before he did, he kissed the top of Elise's head and murmured something else in her ear.

Griff was so thankful things had turned out for the best.

But that had been close. Too close.

BETHANY FELT relief wash through her when she saw Griff step inside the cottage. Against her better judgment, she rushed toward him, desperate to confirm everyone was okay.

Before the question could leave her lips, Griff asked, "How's my little girl?"

"She's fine. Maybe even a little sleepy." Bethany switched her daughter to her other hip as the girl's body began to feel limp with exhaustion against hers. "How are Colton and Elise?"

"They're safe."

Bethany let out a long breath. Thank God.

"What happened to the guy?" Benjamin looked stiff as he joined them, like anger had made his muscles go ramrod straight. "Does Colton need me downstairs?"

"Colton is fine right now," Griff said. "The man . . . he's dead. CJ shot him. Right in time, too."

"CJ?" Benjamin questioned.

Griff nodded. "That's right. She saved Elise's life."

Bethany would ask who CJ was at another time. Whoever the woman was, she sounded fascinating.

"What about the drone?" Benjamin continued. "Is it still there?"

"CJ shot it down," Griff said. "At least we'll be able to examine it. Maybe we can even get an ID on this guy. All in all, things could have turned out a lot worse."

"I can't believe it happened." Bethany shook her head as shock continued to course through her.

"None of us can," Griff said.

"Why try to take Elise and Ada?" Bethany said.

"Why not grab Benjamin after they knocked him out? No offense, Benjamin."

"No offense taken," he said. "I'm going to go check out things downstairs, though. You two okay?"

"We'll be fine." Griff turned back to Bethany, not missing a beat in their conversation. "If they have someone we love, we'll be much more likely to bend to their commands. I hate to admit it, but it's the only thing that makes sense."

Bethany's head began to swirl, and she lowered herself to the couch. As she did, Ada scrambled from her arms, suddenly awake. She ran over to her dad. Griff picked her up, and a huge smile stretched across his face. The drama was temporarily forgotten as they embraced.

But not for Bethany. She rubbed her hands on her jeans. It would take a while for all of this to sink in.

"What do we do now?" Bethany asked. "I'd say we should stay here in the house this whole time, but I'm not sure it would do any good."

"I can't argue with that." Griff bounced Ada in his arms, trying to keep her still. "All I can say is that we all need to remain on guard. These guys are smart, and I doubt they're ready to give up yet."

Bethany rubbed her forehead, a headache

coming on. "How did members of the Savages even get into the US?"

"We can only assume that they were planted here. Maybe you've heard the term 'sleeper agents'? That's essentially what they are."

"You have any idea what their plan is?" Bethany continued, desperate to get answers.

"We're still trying to figure all of that out. But so much of the information is classified. Trying to find answers now that none of us are in the military is complicated."

She pulled a pillow onto her lap. "I don't know how much longer I can live like this. It's only been a day, and I already feel like I'm losing my mind."

Griff sat down beside her, Ada still in his arms. "We're going to figure this out, Bethany. I promise you."

Bethany wished she could feel as confident.

CHAPTER ELEVEN

THE POLICE SWARMED beneath the house, documenting the scene. It didn't appear that CJ would be charged in the man's death considering the circumstances around it.

An hour after everything had happened, Bethany handed Ada over to Benjamin and headed downstairs. The police needed to know if she could identify the man.

Griff walked beside her, almost as if he was afraid her legs might buckle.

Maybe they would.

As soon as she stepped onto the driveway, Bethany remembered seeing that man who tried to abduct Ada. Remembered the fear she'd felt while thinking about her little girl being taken away.

Part of her wanted to curl up in a ball and tuck herself away from the world.

But Bethany hadn't been taught to do that. She'd been taught to keep her chin up and be strong.

That's exactly what she intended on being right now.

Nerves claimed her muscles as she paused in front of the man's body. It was covered with a white sheet, and a man with ruddy skin and rust-colored hair stood over it. He stepped out of the way when he spotted Bethany, and Police Chief Cassidy Chambers—Ty's wife—took his place. Bethany had met her during breakfast that morning.

"You ready?" Cassidy eyeballed her with concern, as if trying to ascertain her mental state.

Bethany nodded, though she didn't know if she'd ever truly be ready.

As Cassidy slowly pulled the sheet back, a face stared at Bethany.

She sucked in a breath.

This was the man from the park.

He had followed her to Lantern Beach, and he'd tried to snatch Ada again.

She wished his death might indicate this nightmare was over. But she knew that was far from the truth.

GRIFF WAS STILL LOST in his thoughts an hour later as he paced inside the cottage.

The police had come to gather evidence. The medical examiner showed up. Everything had been documented. All of them had been questioned.

A motorcycle had been found in the marsh. Obviously, the man had planned on using it to get away. Knowing that motorcycle had been meant for only one person sent a spike of anger through Griff.

The man hadn't intended on taking Elise or Ada with him.

He'd intended on killing them.

Cassidy had taken the drone as evidence. She was looking for someone who might be able to examine it for them. Maybe the device would offer them information.

But if that man had Elise and Ada, that meant that someone else was operating the drone. Most likely, that person was still on the island. They had to track down the location these people were operating out of.

None of that had made him feel any better.

Dez and Ty were also back and had gotten the update. The car down at the ferry—the one belonging to the man who'd jumped into the water—had been registered to someone named Mark Blankenship. The man was thirty-six, he was born in Maryland, and he worked for an electronics store. He had no prior record.

But he did have some pictures of Ada stuffed in his glove compartment—pictures that had been taken at her daycare.

Griff was never going to let Ada go back to that place. Not if he could help it.

As CJ busied herself making lunch, Bethany sat at the kitchen table, still looking dazed. She'd seen those pictures and knew what was going on.

Griff lowered himself across from her, his thoughts still racing. "Was there anyone suspicious at Ada's daycare?"

She looked up, her gaze tumultuous. "Suspicious? I don't know." She shrugged. "I guess Sal could be a little strange."

Griff exchanged a look with Benjamin, who lingered by the door. "Sal who?"

"Sal Philips. He worked there. He's probably in his early twenties, and he loved Ada. He even offered to watch her after hours if I ever needed a sitter."

Hearing her words caused Griff's muscles to tighten even more. "You didn't let him?"

"Sal?" Bethany made a face. "No. Of course not. You know how particular I am."

Griff turned to Benjamin. "Can you do me a favor? Go run this guy's name and see what you can find out about him."

"Sure thing." Benjamin rubbed his head as he walked away.

Doc Clemson—the town doctor and medical examiner—had checked Benjamin out when he came by to examine the dead body. He'd said Benjamin was fine.

That had been a small dose of good news, at least.

Benjamin had become almost like a little brother to Griff over the past couple years. Griff knew that some of the other guys on the team still kept the man at arm's length. He had been the newest member of their SEAL platoon, and because of that, their bond with Benjamin hadn't been as strong. The fact that his uncle had been their commander also made things more tricky.

Griff saw a lot of potential in Benjamin and wanted to help him develop that potential. But Benjamin still had a way to go. The man could be quiet sometimes when he needed to speak, when the guys needed to know they could trust him. It made it seem like Benjamin was keeping secrets.

Griff really hoped that wasn't the case.

"You think Sal is involved with this?" Bethany continued.

Griff looked at the pictures on the table. "A couple of these look like they were taken inside the daycare. I'm telling you, the lengths these guys will go to . . . they won't stop at anything."

Bethany frowned. "In other words, the person behind this might be someone I know."

Griff said nothing, which was answer enough.

CHAPTER TWELVE

A FEW MINUTES LATER, sandwiches, chips, and fruit salad had been placed on the table, and everyone was called together to eat. In spite of everything that had happened, they still needed to keep up their energy. But the mood around the table was quiet and tense, like they were all caught in their own thoughts.

Benjamin had made a call to the daycare, but he hadn't heard back yet. In the meantime, he glanced at the kitchen. "Have you ever thought about cleaning while you cook instead of afterward?"

"Why does it matter to you? You don't clean." CJ raised her eyebrows.

He shrugged. "I'm just saying. It makes more sense."

"Maybe to you." CJ popped a chip in her mouth. "There's more than one way to skin a cat."

Benjamin and CJ had rubbed each other the wrong way since they'd met. Griff found all of it entirely too entertaining. As soon as CJ walked into a room, Benjamin practically became a different person.

Maybe it was because Dez had joked with him, saying the two should date. Or it could be the fact that Benjamin and CJ had been thrown together at more than one event, especially as everyone else had paired off.

Griff knew better—he avoided those situations.

"What is on this sandwich?" Benjamin asked.

"What? Are you going to complain about that now, cowboy?" CJ shot back.

"Something just tastes different." He examined the ham and cheese.

"I added some sriracha to the mayo."

"Why would you do that?"

"Because it tastes good."

"You save the day once, and now you think you have free reign of the sriracha."

CJ gave him a look. "We're really not having this conversation, are we?"

Bethany and Griff exchanged a smile.

Griff had asked Benjamin once about why he let CJ rub him the wrong way. He'd said there was something he didn't trust about CJ. But Griff had to wonder if there was more to it than that.

As much as Griff would like to pretend that this was just a casual lunch, he knew it wasn't. It was evident by looking at everyone around the table that their thoughts were still on what had just happened.

Griff took a bite of a sandwich, wishing that it tasted good. But nothing would taste good right now. Too much was on the line for him to enjoy himself.

He longed for a minute alone with Bethany to check her emotional state. He knew this was hard on her. But he hadn't had that opportunity to grab her alone yet, and he didn't know when he would.

He only hoped all of this had a happy ending. There was a time in his life when he would've bet everything that good would win over evil. But now, he just didn't know. At least not when it came to this life here on earth.

AFTER LUNCH, Bethany and Elise escaped to the screened-in porch to enjoy some coffee and a nice ocean breeze. Griff had insisted on taking care of

Ada for a little while so that Bethany could get some rest. She wasn't going to argue.

Even though being outside didn't feel like the safest option, they knew Benjamin and Colton were both downstairs cleaning up the crime-scene area and keeping an eye out for trouble. It felt good to be away from everything for a moment and to feel like maybe she and Elise were just two girlfriends catching up on life.

"Are you sure you're okay?" Bethany asked Elise as they sat beside each other on a bench swing. "I'm worried about you."

Elise nodded. But, as she ran a hand through her hair, Bethany saw the tremble claiming her muscles. "I'll be okay. I've been through worse."

Bethany almost didn't want to know what she was talking about. But, based on what Griff had already told her, Elise was not only grieving the loss of her husband but she'd almost been killed too.

"I should be asking you how you're doing," Elise said. "Seeing Ada almost being abducted twice . . . I can only imagine how you're feeling. No mother should have to go through that."

Bethany glanced down at her mug of coffee. "It all seems surreal, that's for sure. I'm just so thankful that everything has turned out okay so far."

"Me too."

Bethany paused the swing as she caught a glimpse of what was happening inside.

On the other side of the screen door, she saw Ada sitting at the table painting Griff's toenails.

"You're doing a fantastic job." Griff stared down at the pink slathered across his toes. "I feel like a million bucks."

Ada beamed up at her dad.

Moisture filled Bethany's eyes.

It was such a beautiful sight.

Griff had always been a great dad. It was why it made no sense when, one day, it seemed like a switch flipped and he decided to walk away from his family. To this day, Bethany still had trouble coming to terms with it. At first, she'd thought he would eventually come to his senses. But, as the months passed, it became clear that wouldn't happen.

"He's a good dad," Elise said beside her.

Bethany crossed her arms over her chest and looked away, so as to not interrupt the moment. "He is. Or was. I'm not sure sometimes."

Elise examined Bethany's face, her expression a good mix of psychologist and friend. "You still love him, don't you?"

"What?" Bethany let out a skeptical laugh and

raked a hand through her hair. "No. That's ridiculous. Griff and I have a child together. We'll always have that bond. But nothing else."

"That's a shame," she said softly. "Because I'm pretty sure he still loves you."

Bethany blinked at Elise's words, unsure if she heard correctly. "Why would you say that? It's ridiculous—no offense. But I've given Griff every opportunity to make things right, and he's obviously very content to be a bachelor."

"No offense taken. But I'm really not sure that's true. It's pretty obvious by the way he looks at you that he cares."

"When you love someone, you don't abandon them." A bitter edge laced Bethany's words. She tried not to feel sorry for herself. She really did. But she still struggled to understand what had gone so wrong between them. Sure, they'd had their issues. Every married couple did. But they should have been able to work them out.

"I don't know what Griff was thinking." Elise shook her head and frowned. "Sometimes, I think he was trying to look out for you. I'm not sure if that makes sense, but... it's just my gut feeling."

Bethany couldn't allow herself to believe that again. The risk was too great. "I just can't see how he would think something like that. What's best for Ada and me would be being a family. At least, it was. We've learned how to manage for ourselves—for the most part."

Elise's expression showed she didn't quite believe that.

Footsteps pounded up the stairs, interrupting them.

Good. Because Bethany didn't want this conversation to go any further.

The last thing she wanted was to justify Griff's actions.

CHAPTER THIRTEEN

GRIFF LOOKED up at Colton and Benjamin as they stepped into the cottage. As Colton glanced over at him, Griff wiggled his toes, which were now painted cotton candy pink.

Colton paused and raised his eyebrows. "Pretty."

"I think so too," Griff said, observing his daughter's handiwork. "Ada did a great job."

"I'd say so. Hey, listen. As soon as your spa day is over, could I steal you for a few minutes?"

"I think she was just wrapping up now, weren't you, Warrior Princess?" Griff leaned toward his daughter and kissed the top of her head.

Ada grinned and put the nail polish back into a plastic carry case. "All done, Daddy. Would you like me to fix your hair now?"

Griff ran his hand through his hair and tried to imagine what Ada might be considering doing with it. Braids? A pink streak? A burst of poofy curls just like his grandmother had sported?

"That will have to be for another day." He looked over and saw Bethany and Elise step back into the cottage. Perfect timing. He looked at Bethany and nodded at Ada. "Do you mind?"

"Of course not," Bethany said. There was a new look on her face—her expression almost looked strained.

What had they been talking about out there? Whatever it was, he couldn't worry about it now.

Griff, Benjamin, and Colton slipped into the office down the hallway. Griff could tell that Colton had something on his mind, just by the way he held his shoulders. They looked stiff and unyielding. What had Colton learned?

"Commander Larson just called back," Colton started.

Griff's breath caught. "And?"

"He acknowledged that it doesn't seem on the surface like a lot has been done to get to the bottom of this situation with the Savages. But he had a reason for it."

Griff couldn't imagine what that might be.

Dealing with terrorists wasn't a matter to be taken lightly or to be put on the back burner. He felt like that was exactly what the commander and secretary were doing.

"They think the traitor who's infiltrated the government could all be at a higher level than Secretary Stabler or Commander Larson," Colton said.

Griff twisted his head. "A higher level?"

"Maybe even at cabinet level."

"The president's cabinet?" The words didn't even sound right leaving Griff's lips.

"Maybe. They don't know if it goes up that high. It could be within the CIA or Homeland Security. But they do feel that there's still someone on the inside who's feeding these guys information, someone other than Jason."

"So they're staying quiet about it for that reason?" Griff tried to give them the benefit of the doubt.

"They're trying to keep a low profile until they can figure things out. Right now, they don't know whom they can trust."

"Did he tell you anything of value?" Griff tried to respect the way they were trying to handle the situation, but he had expected more from them.

"They do believe that these guys are planning

some sort of attack." Colton's voice hardened, as if all this had upset him—and rightfully so. "They are trying to listen to the scuttlebutt around what's going on. The CIA has shared some intel with them, and there have been other missions the SEALs have been deployed on to try to bring these guys down. But there hasn't been any success with that yet."

"That's a shame, to put it lightly."

"I agree. At this point, I guess what they want us to do is to trust them, to believe that they're doing their jobs."

Griff stared up at Colton. "What are you going to do?"

"I can't help but think that the person behind the events of the past couple days is a minion, for lack of a better word, for someone else. I feel like someone else is pulling the strings and telling these other guys what to do. We need to find that person."

"And you think Jason was one of those minions too, don't you?"

"I do."

If that was the case, they were just skimming the surface here. "Any guesses as to who the puppet master might be?"

"No, but I have to wonder who else might be helping this person. Because it's bigger than one rogue agent or member of the military. There's an entire network of these people who are working for the Savages. Maybe even someone we know or someone we've worked with."

"Like who?"

Colton let out a long breath. "There are definitely people on the inside. Maybe another SEAL. Leonardo is still a suspect in my mind."

"Leonardo?" Griff questioned.

Another SEAL had shown up in Lantern Beach a few months ago, out of the blue, and had asked for a job with Blackout. Griff had to admit that Leonardo wasn't his favorite person. But they hadn't seen him in town for a while. Still, could the man have been sent here to gather information?

"My guess is that they may have even planted someone close to Bethany," Colton said.

"She did mention someone named Sal Philips. Benjamin is looking into him." He turned toward his friend. "Speaking of which . . . any updates?"

"Sal didn't show up for work today," Benjamin announced. "And he's been having financial troubles."

Griff and Colton exchanged a look.

"We definitely need to look into this more,"

Colton said. "In the meantime, anyone else? Maybe a coworker who has ties to the military."

Griff's mind raced. "Bethany's friend Cindi . . . her husband is in the military."

"Did he set off any red flags?" Colton asked.

"He's always seemed a little strange. He's hard to read, to say the least. Bethany is close with his wife."

"Maybe we should look into his background also, just to be safe," Colton said.

"Good idea. But why not let the commander and Secretary Stabler figure it out?" Griff asked, anxious to hear his leader's response.

"Because what if they're wrong?"

Colton's question hung in the air. It was a valid one. And it matched Griff's instincts.

With stakes this high, they couldn't take any chances.

THE REST of the day had been a blur. They'd played games with Ada and tried to keep her occupied. They'd had dinner together. Everything felt normal, but Bethany knew it was anything but normal.

She was halfway relieved when nighttime finally

fell, and it was time to get Ada to sleep. She, Griff, and Ada had gone to the cabana together. It had only taken ten minutes for her daughter to fall asleep. She was obviously exhausted.

With Ada snoozing on the bed and Griff in the shower, Bethany slipped outside. She just needed a moment alone.

Everything was hitting her. The shock was wearing off, and, instead, the grim reality of what had happened weighed on her shoulders.

Ada had almost been snatched. Twice.

If just one thing had been different in each situation Ada might not be here right now.

Bethany waved to the man standing guard, silently asking for privacy. He wore a police uniform, so Cassidy must have sent him to take over duty for a while. Bethany would have to introduce herself later, when she felt more social.

The officer seemed to get the message and slipped around the corner. He remained on guard, but not in her space. Thankfully.

She sucked in a breath, breathing in the fresh salt air. Above her, the stars shone brightly. The breeze felt cool and comforting. It was almost like nature knew Bethany needed a few of her favorite things right now.

Finally alone, tears streamed down her cheeks. The emotions she'd held inside released themselves in a whoosh that reminded Bethany of a crashing wave. She wanted to be strong—she *had* to be strong for Ada—but she'd be lying if she didn't admit she was scared.

Terrified, for that matter.

Her little girl had come so close to being snatched. Ada meant everything in the world to Bethany. If something had happened to her . . . Bethany wasn't sure how she could go on.

The door creaked open behind her, and she glanced back.

Griff.

Quickly, Bethany wiped the moisture from her face and tried to compose herself.

But she couldn't. The sob she tried to hold back escaped louder than ever—from deep in her gut, her soul, her heart.

The next instant, Griff was behind her. His arms wrapped around her, and he pulled her close while murmuring in her ear, "It's okay to cry."

Something about hearing him give her permission caused a dam to break inside her. More tears flowed down her cheeks, and cries wracked her body.

Griff held her closer, his arms strong and familiar. Bethany didn't want to find comfort in him . . . but, despite herself, she did.

He understood. He'd almost lost his daughter too.

As angry as she was at the man, as much as she wanted to believe he didn't care . . . she knew he did. He was just so confusing to her. Distant one minute. Looking at her with so much concern the next.

Bethany had to remind herself that this man had left her. He'd left Ada. He'd chosen a different life and given up on their vows.

She couldn't pretend he hadn't.

Getting used to Griff being around wasn't in her best interest . . . or Ada's. In the end, it would just lead to more heartache.

That was something she couldn't afford.

Bethany sucked in a long breath and used the sleeve of her sweatshirt to wipe beneath her eyes.

Then she stood and turned toward Griff. "Thank you, but . . . I should get inside. It's been a long day."

An unreadable expression crossed his gaze until he finally nodded. "Of course."

She fled, trying to forget just how good it had felt to be in his arms.

That was easier said than done.

CHAPTER FOURTEEN

GRIFF COULDN'T SLEEP. He had too many things running through his mind. So much had happened today. Too much.

Instead, he lay on his cot and let the facts race through his mind.

He was a solutions guy. He liked to come up with a plan, execute it, and find success. But in this situation, it was hard to see what the plan might be. He didn't like that.

He fought a smile as he remembered the feeling of holding Bethany in his arms. He hadn't intended on doing it. No, he'd intended on staying away for a long time. Forever, for that matter.

But that phone call two days ago had changed everything. He'd known when he saw both Bethany and Ada again that he loved them more than anything in this whole world. Could he ever make them understand why he'd had to leave?

And, even if he did explain, none of it seemed to matter anymore. Here they were, and they were in danger. This was the last thing that he'd wanted—the very thing he'd tried to avoid.

Griff closed his eyes again. Remembered the feel of Bethany in his arms. Remembered the sweet scent of her shampoo. Remembered feeling her soft skin against his.

His heart hammered in his chest. He'd missed that connection. He had missed Bethany. So much.

How was he going to get through this situation unscathed? Not only was he concerned about their safety, but he knew that, at the end of all this, he could be in a very dark place.

Maybe he would take Elise up on that offer to talk. Maybe he needed someone with whom to share his deepest secrets, to share the pieces of his heart that he'd tried to hide permanently.

He turned over again, wishing sleep would find him. Even though a guard was stationed outside the cabana, Griff couldn't help but listen for any signs of trouble. The guys behind this were good. They were professionals. They would do whatever was necessary to get their hands on Ada.

Anger rushed through his veins. Griff couldn't let anybody hurt Ada. Or Bethany.

He would do whatever it took to protect them, even if it meant sacrificing himself.

BETHANY JERKED AWAKE, an internal alarm alerting her that something was wrong. Her heart raced and sweat spread across her skin as she glanced around.

"Help!" Ada yelled beside her, thrashing on the bed.

Ada was having a nightmare, she realized.

Just a nightmare.

Across the room, Griff sprang forward, looking instantly on alert.

"It's okay," Bethany mouthed, pointing down at Ada.

His shoulders seemed to soften when he saw that Ada was safe. He ran a hand over his face.

"Daddy!" She suddenly sat up in bed, tears running down her cheeks. "Daddy! Daddy! Daddy!"

Griff rose to his feet and rushed to her side.

Not wearing a shirt again, Bethany noted.

That was a conversation for later, though.

He knelt by the bed. As he did, Ada threw her arms around him, and he pulled her close.

"What's wrong with my girl?"

"I had a bad dream, Daddy." Ada clung to him, tears pouring down her face. "I was so scared."

"It's going to be okay," he murmured. "I'm right here."

Bethany watched the exchange. Ada had asked for her dad again. That fact wasn't lost on Bethany. Ada desperately wanted her father in her life, and everything that had happened over the past year hadn't changed that. She used to wake up asking for Griff at least a few times a week.

But the even bigger issue at hand was the fact that the events of the past couple days were taking a toll on her daughter, weren't they? Ada was terrified. Bethany could try to protect Ada all she wanted, but the damage had already been done.

Remorse ached in Bethany's chest with every beat of her heart. She didn't want Ada to be caught in the crossfire. To be a victim of choices her little girl had never even made. The fact that these Savages were targeting Ada was reprehensible.

Griff cradled Ada to his chest until her eyes

started to droop. Ada had found safety in her father's arms.

A moment later, Griff lifted her and put her back in bed beside Bethany. Just before he removed his arms from around her, Ada's eyes flung open and she grabbed Griff.

"Don't leave, Daddy. Please." Ada sniffled, as if on the verge of tears again.

Griff exchanged a glance with Bethany, silently asking her what to do.

Bethany scooted over until her back hit the wall. When she did, Griff slid into bed beside Ada. The girl cuddled up beside her father and fell back to sleep.

She and Griff exchanged another look.

Bethany's heart continued to pound in her chest. She was all too aware of how close Griff was. Of how cozy this arrangement was. Of how this felt entirely too normal.

It was like they were all playing family again.

Yet, as she lay there, she knew that oceans separated her and Griff. Not only oceans, but broken dreams that had been crushed by ruthless waves. Good memories that faded faster than the sunset.

Love was supposed to win.

Instead, Bethany felt like a failure. Every time

she looked at Griff, she remembered that. Remembered how divorce was never supposed to be in their vocabulary. Yet it was.

Maybe it was Griff's job that had worn them down. The vast amount of time they'd spent apart. Maybe she hadn't been the woman Griff had needed her to be. She didn't know.

For that matter, Griff hadn't been the man she'd expected him to be. All the naysayers—the people who'd warned Bethany against marrying him—had appeared to be right. She'd been wrong.

As she stared at him now, she realized that this situation was going to end badly. Very, very badly. And she had no idea how to prepare herself or Ada for the aftermath.

CHAPTER FIFTEEN

GRIFF TRIED to pretend that everything was normal the next morning as he, Bethany, and Ada headed across the lot and into the cottage. Ty had invited them over for breakfast, and Griff was never one to refuse free food. Plus, he thought it was a good idea to put some space between him and Bethany.

She had been casting dirty looks at him all morning. Apparently, she didn't appreciate what happened last night. But he would have never stayed with Ada if Bethany hadn't given him permission.

Feeling Ada curl up to him brought back so many memories. Too many memories. It made Griff long for things he couldn't have. Now he had to figure out what to do about that.

Inside the cottage, the smell of bacon and eggs and crispy hash browns filled the air. It was a breakfast meant for people who did hard labor. Speaking of which, Griff needed to squeeze in some exercise time or eating like this would undo all the effort that he'd put into staying fit. In his line of work, that was a must.

CJ was at the helm in the kitchen, and Benjamin helped her. But Griff could tell that Benjamin was not enjoying himself. It wasn't even that they bickered, which made it even more funny to Griff.

Benjamin just kept giving her dirty looks, and CJ seemed oblivious to it all. She went about her merry way without giving the man a second thought.

Good. Maybe Benjamin could use a little dose of humility.

The conversation at breakfast felt light and easy. If Griff let himself, he might even be able to imagine that this was just a casual get together among friends. But he knew it was anything but that. There were serious issues at stake here, and he couldn't forget that. He knew that none of them could or would.

As soon as they finished, Griff asked if Colton, Dez, and Benjamin could meet in the office for a minute. He'd just finished a phone call a few minutes ago, and he wanted to share the information he'd learned. He was anxious to hear if Colton had any updates as well.

Once in the room, no one bothered to sit. Instead, they stood in a circle facing each other, waiting to hear what Griff and Colton had to say.

"I got a call from Anderson this morning," Griff started. "He told me that another SEAL team was on a mission a few days ago—a mission that involved the Savages."

"And?" Colton asked.

"The SEAL team captured a man who'd been injured in a blast. He wasn't quite in his right mind. But apparently, he told them that there was 'more coming and that the finger was on the trigger.'"

Dez pulled his shoulders up in a stiff shrug. "What does that mean?"

"I can only assume it means that whatever the Savages are planning, it's imminent," Griff said.

"Did this terrorist say anything else?" Benjamin asked.

"He also said the word 'revenge,'" Griff said.

"What does that mean?" Colton asked.

"No idea." Griff shrugged.

"I don't like this." Colton crossed his arms, his entire body appearing tense. "I feel like the tide is rising, and we need answers before we all go under. I have no doubt in my mind that this man would have killed Elise earlier if CJ hadn't arrived when she did."

"Speaking of which, who sent that text to her?" Griff asked. The question had haunted him all night.

Colton's face tightened again. "I have no idea. We can try to trace the number, but I have a feeling it won't turn up anything. Whoever it was, it looks like we have a guardian watching out for us."

"If this person is a guardian, why isn't he or she showing their face?" Griff didn't like secrets like that. They only led to trouble.

"I have no idea. But we know what we need to do. We continue to look into Sal Philips. We look into Cindi's husband. We find out as much information as we can on this man who died yesterday. Above all, we keep the people we love safe. Understood?"

"Understood," they all muttered.

But Griff didn't feel any better. In fact, if anything, he felt worse.

BETHANY PATIENTLY WAITED for Griff to finish with his meeting.

They had another emergency to attend to—only this one wasn't the life or death type. This was a parenting emergency.

Breakfast had already been cleaned up. They had read a story to Ada, and CJ had entertained them by juggling spoons. She'd offered to juggle knives, but nobody thought that that was a good idea. Then Ada had munched on some raisins.

That's where their emergency had started.

Finally, Bethany heard the office door open, and she waved Griff over. "Ada put a raisin up her nose."

Ada frowned as she sat in the kitchen chair. Her chin trembled. The poor girl was so upset. Bethany and CJ had tried everything they could to get the raisin out.

Griff knelt in front of Ada. "You know, those taste a lot better if you put them in your mouth instead."

Ada nodded, her eyes filling with tears.

Griff leaned closer, examining her nose. Finally, he leaned back and shook his head. "I think we're going to need to take her to the clinic. Maybe Doc Clemson can get that out. I'm afraid I'm going to push it up farther."

Bethany nodded. "That's what I figured. Is it safe to leave?"

"It will have to be."

Bethany stood and reached for Ada's hand. "Come on, sweet girl. We'll get this taken care of."

A few minutes later, they were in Griff's truck, headed down the road.

Each time she remembered the rush of feeling like she, Griff, and Ada were all a family, the feeling was immediately replaced by regret.

She couldn't let Griff back into her life. The smartest thing she could do was to be cordial but keep the distance between them.

It only took a few minutes to drive to the clinic, and they were taken back to a room right away. The doc was going to be with them as soon as he finished seeing another patient. In the meantime, a kind nurse brought Griff and Bethany some coffee, and Ada a juice box.

"Mommy, Daddy," Ada started as she sat on the examination table with a frown on her face.

"What is it, sweetie?" Griff asked.

"I want a baby brother or sister."

Bethany nearly spit her coffee out. Instead, she swallowed the hot brew—a little too quickly, which led to a coughing fit.

Griff raised an eyebrow. "Are you okay?"

She hit her chest with her fist and nodded. "Just fine. You take that one."

Griff turned back to Ada. "A little brother or sister would be fun, huh?"

"Griff . . ." That wasn't what he was supposed to say.

He raised a hand, as if saying to give him a chance. "But I don't think that's going to happen, sweetie."

Ada frowned again. "I miss you, Daddy."

Griff squeezed her hand, all of his earlier glib gone. "I know, honey. I miss you too."

Bethany looked away before anyone could see the heartbreak in her eyes.

Ada had just stopped asking about her dad so much.

When this was over, Ada was going to have to adjust to his absence again.

Bethany's heart ached at the thought of it.

CHAPTER SIXTEEN

AS THEY WAITED for the doctor and Ada entertained herself with some tongue depressors, Bethany glanced at her phone. She frowned at an email that she saw there.

Griff glanced over her shoulder. "What is it?"

She shook her head. "Nothing, probably. It's just that I got a message from my boss that doesn't make much sense."

"What's it say?"

She blinked to make sure that she was seeing things correctly before reading the email. *Bethany, I'm asking all the employees to sign this document below. It's very important. I know you are taking a leave of absence right now, but if you can get this done ASAP, that would be great. Thank you, John Epstein.*

"What's so strange about that?"

She shrugged. "I know it probably doesn't make much sense, but my boss has never sent an email like this before. I can't imagine what this might be, and I'm hesitant to click on the link."

"Why don't you call him first and make sure it's legit? We probably have a few minutes still until Doc Clemson will be here."

"Good idea." Bethany dialed his number. John answered on the second ring.

"Bethany! I didn't expect to hear from you. I hope everything is well."

She didn't know how to respond to that, so she pretended like she didn't hear and jumped to the heart of the matter. "I'm calling about this email that you just sent."

"Email?"

"The one where you asked me to sign a document. Something about it didn't sit right with me, so I just wanted to make sure you had really sent it."

He paused for a beat. "When did you get this email?"

"Just now. It said you sent it two hours ago."

He let out a grunt. "I can assure you that I have not sent any emails out asking for any signatures. Perhaps it's a phishing email."

"Perhaps. But it did come from your address, and it does have my name, and it's even spelled correctly. Plus, my leave of absence was mentioned." The message definitely had a personal touch.

"Do me a favor and forward that to me. I'll have our IT guys check into it, just to make certain there's not something suspicious going on."

"Sure thing. I'll do that as soon as I get off the phone." Maybe his team could find some answers. If they did, it would make Bethany feel better.

"I'll be looking for it. Take care of yourself, Bethany."

She ended the call, and, before she forgot, forwarded the email to her boss. When she was done with that, she glanced back at Griff. He stared at Ada, the look in his eyes full of longing.

Bethany cleared her throat, trying to regain her focus. "John said it's probably just some phishing email. You know we all get those all the time."

Griff's gaze narrowed as he turned back to her. "It wasn't written in broken English, however. That is suspicious within itself."

"What are you getting at?" Bethany heard something in his words, something that hinted there could be more to this.

"I'm just saying that, at this point, everything is on the table. Every possibility should be examined."

"You are more than welcome to investigate this email if you would like."

As Bethany looked at him, her cheeks burned again. They kept doing that, and that was not a good sign. But when she remembered Griff sleeping beside Ada, it did something funny to her heart.

She had to get Griff out of her system. Because the situation was only going to get harder.

Thankfully, just then, the doctor came into the room.

GRIFF WAITED for Doc Clemson to find a different pair of forceps to remove the raisin from Ada's nose.

The first one hadn't worked.

He was feeling restless, though. What he really wanted was to be out there looking for the person behind all of this. His first priority had to be keeping his daughter safe, though.

Bethany alternated between playing with Ada and staring off into space, looking like she didn't know what to do with herself.

Griff wished he could take some of her anxiety

away, but he knew that would be a bad idea. That very anxiety could keep her alive.

Finally, a knock sounded at the door. He turned, expecting Clemson to be there. Instead, it was Cassidy.

"I heard you two were here," Cassidy said. "How's that nose, Ada?"

Ada narrowed her eyes and crossed her arms. "Bad."

"I'm so sorry to hear that." Cassidy frowned for Ada before turning back to Griff and Bethany. "I have a little update for you."

"We'd love an update," Griff said.

Cassidy closed the door behind her. "First of all, Brian Starks is awake. Colton and Elise are headed to Raleigh so they can talk to him. I told them I'd pass on that message."

"Good to know," Griff said.

"I also wanted to let you know," Cassidy lowered her voice, "that I got a fingerprint match from that knife found in Ada's bag."

Bethany jerked to her feet and stepped closer. Griff also closed in, eager to hear what Cassidy had to say. Maybe they'd finally have some answers.

"And?" he asked.

"You're never going to believe this." Cassidy's

gaze locked onto his. "The print that we found on the knife matches Jason Perkins."

"Who is Jason Perkins?" Bethany's gaze wavered back and forth from Griff to Cassidy.

"Jason is the person I told you about, the one who worked for the commander as a driver," Griff explained. "He's the one who came after Elise. He's in jail now."

Bethany's eyes narrowed. "But if he's in jail . . . how did his knife get in the bag?"

"That's what we are all wondering." Cassidy frowned.

"What about the blood?" Griff remembered the gruesome sight of it, dried on the edges of the weapon. A knife by itself he might be able to excuse as an instrument someone kept in their pocket. The blood took it to an entirely new level.

Cassidy shifted and let out a breath. "We had that tested as well. I was thinking that it would probably be fake blood or animal blood. As it turns out, it's human."

Bethany gasped and put her hand over her mouth. As she did, Ada wandered over and lifted her arms. Bethany picked her daughter up and held her close.

This wasn't her world. She lived in books and

park dates and sunshine. Griff, on the other hand, lived with danger, injury, and backstabbing. He wished he could protect her from all of that.

But this one did have him puzzled. How had Jason's prints gotten on that knife? And exactly whose blood was that?

The mystery around all of this continued to deepen.

Griff shifted, more anxious than ever to find some answers. "What's next?"

"I actually got permission to talk to Jason," Cassidy said. "I'm going to head up to the prison where he's being kept. I want to find out for myself how his prints got on this knife. Maybe he'll have some answers."

"Homeland Security or the FBI is going to approve this visit?" Griff knew how these things worked. A small-town police chief was considered the low person on the totem pole in situations like this.

"They may try to stop me, but I'm going to see what I can do until then."

"Good luck. I hope you're able to find out something." Griff meant the words. Though he wished he could be the one out there talking to Jason, he knew that Cassidy would do a good job. She was tough when she needed to be tough.

As Cassidy disappeared from the room, Griff's thoughts raced. Just what was going on here? What else did he need to do to ensure that Bethany and Ada were safe from all this craziness?

CHAPTER SEVENTEEN

A FEW MINUTES LATER, the raisin had been successfully removed from Ada's nose, and the three of them were sent on their way.

Bethany was grateful to be out of the clinic and on her way back to the cottage.

As they headed down the road, her phone rang. It was her friend Cindi. As Ada happily looked at a book in the backseat, Bethany answered.

Bethany had sent her friend a quick text before she'd left for Lantern Beach. Since the two of them worked together, Cindi needed to know that Bethany wouldn't be in. Knowing Cindi, she'd send the entire police department out looking for her otherwise.

"Cindi," Bethany muttered. "How are you?"

"It's not me that I want to talk about. It's you.

How are you holding up? I can't stop thinking about what happened at the park."

Bethany considered how to honestly answer that question. The past couple of days had been crazy. "I've been better, but I'm still alive so I can't complain."

Cindi chuckled, but it sounded half-hearted. "That's one way to look at it. You've been on my mind. I've been worried about you. And Ada."

"Thanks, but we're doing fine. For now."

"Where are you?"

Bethany froze for a moment, wondering if she should answer. But whoever was chasing her obviously knew that she was here on Lantern Beach. Even if her phone line was somehow bugged, she wasn't going to tell anybody something that they did not already know.

"I came to Lantern Beach," she said. "It's safe here. Safer than it is at home, at least."

"Lantern Beach? Isn't that where your ex is?"

Bethany glanced at Griff. His gaze was focused on the road ahead.

"Yes, it is. But it's all good. Nobody loves Ada like her parents."

"If he loves her so much, why did he leave her?" Cindi gasped as soon as the question left her lips.

"Oh, Bethany. I shouldn't have said that. I'm so sorry."

Bethany felt the frown forming on her face. The question had felt like a slap, but maybe it was what she needed to hear. "No, you're right. That's a question that I've asked myself also."

"Has it been awkward?"

Bethany stole a quick glance at Griff. "You could say that. But you know I'll do anything for Ada. Even put up with Griff."

"Hey, I heard that," Griff muttered.

Bethany smiled briefly. She'd said it loud enough that he could hear, just to give him a hard time.

"I'll be praying for all of you," Cindi continued. "When this is all over, I want to hear about it."

When this is all over . . . sometimes, Bethany didn't feel like it would ever be over. The stress of the situation made the days feel more like years and, as far as she was concerned, there was no end in sight.

Despite that, she said, "Thank you."

"And, not to change the subject, but you'll never believe who called me this morning," Cindi continued.

"Who's that?"

"Mason."

Bethany paused, trying to figure out where this

was going. Certainly Cindi wasn't going to play matchmaker now, of all times. "Why would Mason call you?"

"He noticed that you didn't come home the past two nights. He got worried."

Bethany tucked a leg beneath her. "I didn't even know he had your number."

"Remember that party you had at your house at Christmas time? We talked while we were there, and it turned out he was looking for a dog trainer. He gave me his number so I could text him the name of the lady we used for FiFi."

"Oh, I see." Her explanation made sense. "That was kind of him to notice. It's always good to be missed."

"That's why people say that you need nosy neighbors." Cindi's voice lilted up in a brittle laugh.

Bethany stared out the window, marveling at the weathered landscape on the barrier island. She only wished she was here solely to enjoy it. "What did you tell him?"

"I told him that you were shaken up over what happened, but that you were fine. That you just needed to get away for a few days."

Still, Bethany tried to put all the pieces together. Maybe she was just overthinking things. But whoever was behind this had been watching her. Knew her schedule. The more information she had, the better her chances of figuring out how to protect her daughter.

"I know I told you this earlier, but I think Mason really cares about you, Bethany. When this is all over, maybe you should give him a shot. Even Ian likes him."

Ian was Cindi's husband. He was a captain in the military, and one of those strong, silent types.

"Good to know."

"Even Ian has been concerned, by the way. He asked where you were. When I told him you were with Griff, he said you could stay with us. He'd even drive and pick you up himself."

"I appreciate the offer, but I'm fine."

As Ada fussed in the backseat, Griff began singing her a song and making silly faces in the mirror.

This was what Bethany had imagined for her future. Ada growing up with a mom and dad who loved her and were there for her.

Why did it have to take an emergency to make it happen? Even more so, she had to remind herself that this was not permanent. Soon enough, both she and Griff would return to their normal lives. And

Bethany would have to take some proactive steps to move on.

Bethany remembered what Cindi said about giving Mason a chance. She'd known the man was interested. Had heard him hinting that maybe they could get together sometime. She'd always pretended she didn't notice.

"I'll think about it," Bethany said. Maybe it *was* time for her to move on—after she got her official divorce papers, of course.

"That's my girl," Cindi said. "Now, you take care of yourself. If you need anything at all, you give me a call. I don't know what I can do, but I have been brushing up on my ninja skills."

That got a laugh out of Bethany. "You're first on my list if I need help, Cindi. Thanks so much for offering."

GRIFF TRIED NOT to listen to too much of the conversation, but he couldn't help it.

There was something he just didn't like about Bethany's neighbor. The man had moved in two and a half years ago, back when he and Bethany were still together. Even back then, he'd rubbed Griff the wrong way.

Maybe it was the fact that Mason had always been so helpful to Bethany whenever Griff had been deployed. Griff supposed he should be grateful, but he'd never gotten to that point.

And there was more to it than that. It was also the fact that Mason seemed like exactly the kind of guy Bethany *should have* ended up with. The man had a stable job, an even temperament, and he was active in his church. Griff, on the other hand, had baggage, had an erratic work schedule, and he hadn't gone to church until he had met Bethany.

Bethany changed everything. From the moment they had met, Griffin had known he wanted to be a better man. The kind of man who was worthy of someone like Bethany. And when she had said yes to that first date . . . he'd been walking on the clouds.

When that first date had gone well, Griff had felt even more elated. Their relationship had felt relatively seamless, other than the protest Bethany had received from her family. They'd been worried Griff would corrupt her. He supposed when he'd left her, all their concerns had felt justified.

But hearing Bethany talking to Cindi just now

had done something strange to his heart. It made him realize that Bethany had moved on. She had friends. She had other men who were interested in her.

Had she dated? He didn't think so. But the thought of it made his heart twist.

No, that's what you want. You want the best for her. You're not the best.

Mentally, he might understand that. But emotionally? He couldn't stand the thought of her being with anyone else.

Days like today made him realize what he was missing out on. The ordinary things like taking your child to the clinic for a raisin up her nose.

He hid a smile.

Ada could definitely be a handful at times. But children who marched to their own beat, who were strong-willed . . . they were the ones who could change the world.

As they came upon a bend in the road, Griff pressed on the brakes.

Nothing happened.

His adrenaline surged.

He pressed again.

Still nothing.

"What's going on?" Bethany asked.

He swallowed hard. "The brakes aren't working."

"That's . . . not good."

"No, it's not."

As an eighteen-wheeler—probably from the hotel site—came toward them, he braced himself and tried to figure out a plan.

CHAPTER EIGHTEEN

CASSIDY KNOCKED on the office door and waited until she heard Ty say, "Come in." She was pleasantly surprised when she stepped inside and saw Ty by himself looking over the books at his desk.

"How's everything going?" Cassidy closed the door behind her, shutting out the sounds from her living room.

He turned toward her and ran a hand over his face. She knew her husband—he'd much rather be doing something physical any day than doing paperwork. Maybe, in good time, he could hire someone else to help him with administrative work.

"Not too bad," he finally said. "Of course, it would be better if we had more money coming in. I really need to hire somebody to do fundraising for me. It's not my specialty."

"I thought with that donation my father's company made to you, along with Bree's donation, you were all set."

"You would be surprised how much it costs to bring these guys out here for Hope House."

Ty didn't want to burden attendees with any extra expenses, so he paid airfare for everyone who came. But all the costs added up very quickly. Though they were both thrilled to have CJ working here, she was also another expense.

"I know the Blackout guys are looking for somewhere else they can stay," Cassidy said. "Although, I'm not sure if that helps or hurts. I suppose the only thing they're costing us is some food and electricity. I really don't mind having them here."

"But it would be nice to have a little more privacy sometimes, wouldn't it?"

"Yes, it would." Cassidy glanced back at the hallway as she heard CJ singing in the kitchen. It was kind of her thing whenever she cooked. "Especially when we decide to have a family."

She returned her gaze to Ty, watching his expression. They had talked about having kids before, but the subject hadn't been brought up recently. Initially, they had decided to wait at least four years to get established before starting a family. But sometimes, when Cassidy saw little babies and children, her heart panged with a longing she didn't know she had.

First, her friend Rebecca had a baby. Now one of her closest friends, Lisa Dillinger, was pregnant. And seeing Ada here...

Ty stood from his chair and wrapped his arms around Cassidy's waist. "You're really thinking about children?"

She shrugged. "I don't know. I know there would be a lot of benefits to waiting four years—now down to three, by the way. But other times I think, what are we waiting for? There's never going to be an ideal time."

"I agree." He leaned closer until their foreheads touched. "I would be open to the idea of talking about having kids sooner rather than later."

Warmth rushed through Cassidy, and she ran a finger along the side of his face. "Would you? I can't tell you how happy that makes me."

He grinned. "I like making you happy."

"But that's going to have to wait until later." She took a step back.

Ty straightened and tilted his head, his hands still resting on her waist. "What's going on?"

"I've got to go up to Virginia Beach."

Ty squinted. "Virginia Beach? Why Virginia Beach?"

She explained the knife and its connection to Jason Perkins. As soon as she said Jason's name, Ty tensed again.

"I should go with you," Ty said.

"That's not necessary. You have stuff to do here for Hope House."

"But—"

She raised a finger. "No buts about it. I shouldn't be in any danger. I'm just going to go and ask some questions. Besides, I'm kind of looking forward to getting away from all of this drama with the hotel."

That got a small smile out of him. "I can't blame you for that. But I don't want to go with you because you're incapable. I want to go so we can spend time together."

Delight burst inside her. She hoped she never stopped feeling this way about her husband. She thanked God every day He'd brought them together.

Cassidy stepped closer and planted a kiss on Ty's lips. "You convinced me then. Let's go."

CHAPTER NINETEEN

GRIFF STAYED in his lane and eased past the truck.

He released a breath.

First obstacle conquered.

But he still had to figure out how to stop this pickup without anyone getting hurt.

By not pressing the accelerator, his truck slowed. If he could continue decreasing his speed, he could turn down the lane toward Ty's cottage in a few minutes.

He hit the brakes again.

Still nothing.

Someone must have tampered with his truck. But when? While they were at the clinic?

He was going to have to see if they had security

cameras. He found it hard to believe someone was able to do this without being spotted.

"Griff?" Bethany asked.

"I've got this," he murmured.

With her lips pressed together, she nodded. She was nervous. Why wouldn't she be? After everything that had happened, she had to be expecting the worst.

As he approached the lane, he gradually turned the steering wheel. He was going slow enough that he was able to make the turn without going into the ditch.

Score a second victory.

But this wasn't over yet.

The truck was still moving.

A sand dune rose at the end of the lane. If worse came to worst, he could hit it. Impact would be minimal.

Only inches before the dune, the truck rolled to a stop.

He released his breath.

Crisis averted.

For now.

BETHANY CLOSED her eyes as she realized they weren't going to hit the dune.

Thank goodness.

Worst-case scenarios had been running through her mind—scenarios that had ended with someone being hurt.

Who could have cut the brake line? It made no sense.

She couldn't figure out the endgame. Did these men want to abduct Ada? Or did they want to kill them both? It didn't make sense.

And what about what Griff had said? What if the person behind this was someone she knew?

The bad feeling continued to brew in her gut.

On the bright side, Ada was okay. For now, at least.

They hopped out of the truck and stood beneath Ty's place for a minute. While Griff examined the truck, Bethany glanced around, looking for any signs of trouble.

She saw nothing.

For now.

How long would that last?

Griff popped back from beneath the truck a moment later. "Someone definitely cut the brake line, probably while we were in the clinic."

"Whatever we do, these guys are always there, aren't they?"

He frowned. "Yes, they are."

His words didn't make her feel any better, unfortunately.

CHAPTER TWENTY

INSIDE THE HOUSE, Griff turned to Ada, giving her his full attention as they built a tower together. But, as they played, it was obvious that Ada was becoming restless. She was losing patience with the tower, knocking it down. Then she would point outside, like it was driving her crazy not to be exploring.

She'd gotten that from Griff. He'd always loved the outdoors. There was nowhere he felt quite as peaceful.

Bethany had mentioned earlier that Ada liked to throw tantrums lately. He hadn't seen one yet, but he had a feeling his little girl was on the brink right now. Cabin fever seemed to be kicking in.

Bethany watched them from the couch, a frown

on her face. "I wish she could get out there and enjoy the sand and the ocean. Seems like such a shame to be here but stuck inside." She shrugged. "Maybe another time."

Griff glanced at the window. Ada would love the beach. Would love building sandcastles and chasing the waves and entertaining the seagulls.

"If you want to, we can take her on a quick walk."

Bethany's eyes widened as she studied his face. "Are you sure that's safe? Especially after what happened last time..."

"The only thing about being in this cottage is that we're separated from the outside world by four walls. But if someone wants to get to us, it's not these four walls that will save us. It's the people here."

Bethany trembled but remained quiet a moment, as if thinking through his statement.

He meant the words. These guys were ruthless. The walls of this house gave them a false sense of security. Though it might seem like staying inside was the safest option, with the right amount of protection, Griff didn't see anything wrong with venturing outside for a little while. If trouble wanted to find them, then trouble would find them.

"If you don't mind, then, yes, some fresh air sounds nice."

Griff stood. "Let me talk to the guys so we can make sure we have enough eyes on us. I don't think there are very many sand toys here, but hopefully we can make do."

"Just getting outside will be enough," Bethany said. "Fresh air can do a world of good."

Getting outside seemed like just what the doctor ordered. Griff just hoped that he didn't regret it.

BETHANY DREW in a deep breath of the heavy salt-laden air and felt herself relax. The feeling was short-lived, however. Immediately, she turned, looking for any signs of trouble as they walked along the shoreline.

She saw nothing.

The area near Ty's house was away from the tourist area farther down. The only people who used this beach were the ones with little cottages in the area. Since Ty's house sat at the end of that area, his stretch of shoreline was fairly secluded.

She hoped Griff was right and that this was all safe. But she knew that she wouldn't feel safe for a long time. Every time she closed her eyes, the horrifying events of the past few days began replaying again and again.

The drone. Finding Benjamin knocked out. Seeing that man with a gun held to Ada and Elise.

That man was dead, so maybe they'd be safe for a while.

Bethany wished she believed that.

As she and Griff walked beside each other, Ada swung between them, holding each of their hands. Bethany felt the tension stretching between her and her ex. She almost preferred that they bickered to the awkwardness she felt now.

She knew that last night had changed things. Though nothing had happened, it reminded both of them of what had been lost when they had split. Their family had been torn in two, and Ada was the one who would pay the price for that.

Seeing how tender Griff was with Ada didn't do anything to make the situation better. Bethany only wished she could understand why Griff had reacted the way he did. Maybe if she understood, she could feel some peace.

Maybe.

"You and Mason, huh?" Griff glanced over at her.

So he'd heard that part of the conversation.

Bethany shouldn't be surprised. "There is no me and Mason."

Had she just been imagining it or had there been a twinge of jealousy in his voice? She couldn't be sure.

"That's not what it sounded like," Griff said.

"Don't believe everything you hear. He's my neighbor, and that's all."

"But he wants to be more?"

She cast him a sharp glance. "Why does it matter?"

Griff shrugged. "I suppose that it doesn't. Just trying to get a feel for who might be in Ada's life."

Was that why he was asking? Maybe Bethany had misread the jealousy she thought she saw there.

"I suppose you lost the right to have any input when you left us." Bethany rubbed her throat.

She hadn't intended for the words to escape, but they had. Months' worth of emotions had built in her, and this was the first opportunity she had to release them. She always tried to be nicer than necessary, and she thought being blunt would make her feel better.

It didn't. Guilt bit at her instead.

"I guess I deserve that."

"I don't know what to say," Bethany said. "Part of

me thinks I should apologize, but the other part of me knows that I'm only speaking the truth."

"Bethany . . . I wish I could explain. That I *could have* explained. But . . . it's complicated."

"I can understand complicated things." Irritation pinched at her. She was an intelligent woman. She could handle the facts and didn't need to be coddled or protected.

"I wasn't trying to imply that you couldn't. But Bethany—"

Before he could finish what he was saying, Bethany's phone dinged. She expected it to be her boss calling with an update. Instead, it was an unknown number. Despite her better judgment, she clicked on the message.

It was a video. Her eyes widened at what she saw there. The footage had been taken outside her parents' house.

Somebody was watching her mom and dad.

CHAPTER TWENTY-ONE

AS GRIFF LOOKED at the video, his stomach clenched again. The lengths these people had gone to were astounding. Exactly what were they trying to prove? This video seemed to indicate that Bethany was the target.

However, that didn't make any sense.

Bethany squeezed the skin between her eyes and lowered the phone. Her eyes met his. "What should I do?"

Griff had already pulled out his phone. "I have some contacts, some guys I used to work with who are now police officers up in Virginia Beach. I'll give them a call, make sure they go past your parents' house and keep an eye on them."

"Should I call my parents and warn them?"

"It can't hurt to let them know what's going on."

Bethany looked halfway in shock as she nodded and began dialing their number. While they were on the phone, Ada sat on the shoreline and began building mountains out of the sand. Dez and Benjamin stood lookout on either side of them. At the first sign of trouble, they would be out of here.

Griff hoped it didn't come down to that.

After both their calls ended, Griff and Bethany turned to each other. He wanted nothing more than to pull her into his arms and to tell her that everything would be okay. But he couldn't do that. Everything might not be okay.

"What did they say?" Griff asked.

Bethany paused long enough to take a deep breath to compose herself. "They're concerned, of course. But they said they would keep their eyes open. They plan on staying in for the rest of the day anyway."

"That's a good start. We'll make sure the police keep an eye on them as well."

She nodded but didn't look convinced. This was all getting to her, wasn't it?

Griff cleared his throat, determined to distract Bethany from her heavy thoughts. "Your dad still working at the church?"

Bethany stared at Ada, almost absently, and nodded. "He's been there for thirty years now."

"That's great. Is that still where you attend?" Griff knew she did, but he wanted to hear it from her.

"It is. Still singing in the choir, even."

He smiled as he remembered when he'd seen Bethany up there the first time. She'd looked so earnest, so happy. He'd wanted some of that in his own life.

"People got really shaken up when the preacher's daughter came into church with me by her side." Griff remembered the looks they'd gotten when the two of them had walked into a service holding hands for the first time.

That got a small smile out of Bethany. "I know you think I care about what people think, but I really don't. People may have seen a brawny Navy SEAL who'd experienced more of the world in his two decades than most had seen in their lifetimes, but it was never about that for me."

"What did you see?" A lump formed in Griff's throat as he waited for her answer. He shouldn't have asked. He knew better. But he hadn't been able to stop himself.

Bethany's eyes met his. "I saw someone who wanted to change the world. Someone who would overcome incredible obstacles. Someone who had a kind heart behind his tough exterior."

His heart pounded in his ears. She'd always believed in him, hadn't she?

An ache began in Griff's heart at the realization.

Things should have been so different. So, so different.

Was it too late to go back?

Silence fell and that familiar tension stretched between them again. Thank goodness, Ada didn't seem to notice. She happily played in the sand, granules sticking to her skin. But she didn't seem to mind.

Griff wished more than anything that this was just a normal, ordinary day. That he and Bethany were together. That they were on a family vacation to a happy little island.

But nothing could be further from the truth.

He felt Benjamin bristle beside him and followed his friend's gaze.

Farther down the beach, a man walked toward them.

Griff rose to this feet, trying to be cautious.

This could just be a vacationer taking a stroll down the shoreline. But they had to be safe.

Griff exchanged a look with Benjamin and Dez,

and their silent communication made it clear that they were all on the same page. Caution was paramount.

"What is it?" Bethany's voice quivered.

"Probably nothing. We're just being cautious."

But as soon as the words left his mouth, Griff saw another man appear. He came from a crossover about two blocks down. He walked toward them also.

This wasn't a coincidence, Griff realized. Now he had to figure out what he was going to do about it before they had another deadly situation on their hands.

BETHANY FELT HER PULSE RACING. She followed Griff's gaze and saw two men walking their way. Though they wore shorts and T-shirts, there was something strange about them.

Perhaps it was the fact that they were two separate individuals, but both were walking this way by themselves. She didn't know. But if Griff's and his friends' intuition told them this was something to be concerned about, she was also concerned.

She reached for Ada and put a hand on her

shoulder, ready to spring into action. To shield her. She wanted to pull her close.

Who was she kidding?

Bethany wanted to grab her daughter and run. She wanted to escape all of this. She knew that was not possible. Wherever she went, these guys were going to be there.

How long could they live like this? What if this didn't end in a few days? What if the threats continued on and on? What did that mean for her future? For her job?

She had so many questions and so few answers.

Bethany glanced down the shoreline. A third figure appeared. Another male. All three walked toward them. Their steps seemed casual, and she saw no weapons.

Despite that, she could still sense that these guys were dangerous.

"Griff . . ." Her voice trailed as she glanced at him.

Based on the rigid line of his jaw, Griff was taking this very seriously. As were the rest of the guys.

"Should we go after them?" Benjamin asked.

Griff finally said, "That's what they want us to do. I think these guys want to lure us away so they can move in on Bethany and Ada—just like on the ferry."

Another shiver wracked down Bethany's spine.

"So do we just sit here?" Dez's gaze never left the men. "It's your call. Your family."

"We need to start back to the cottage." Griff's hands fisted at his side. "But we move slowly and carefully."

That sounded good to Bethany. She turned toward her daughter. "Ada, we've got to go."

"No . . . !" Her daughter clawed at the sand.

"Ada, this is no time to argue with me. We need to go."

Her daughter dug her hands into the sand and looked up at Bethany with a defiant look in her eyes. "I want to stay!"

Great. Of all the times her daughter had chosen to throw a temper tantrum, it was now.

Bethany didn't have time for this. She scooped down, lifting Ada into her arms.

Her daughter kicked and screamed and reached back for the mound of sand she'd been working on. She wasn't going to make this easy, was she?

Griff cast a glance full of both compassion and concern. He hadn't seen his daughter like this before. It usually only happened when Ada was tired. The girl had definitely been through a lot in the past couple days.

Bethany continued to walk with her daughter toward the cottage, amidst her screams and cries.

"Have you got her?" Griff asked.

She wanted to tell him that she always had Ada. That, as a parent, you didn't walk away. You were there in the good times and bad.

But she held the words back and nodded instead. "I'm good."

She only hoped this situation didn't turn any uglier.

CHAPTER TWENTY-TWO

GRIFF GLANCED behind him again and saw that the three men were still there.

The men had stopped walking and now stared at Griff and his crew. Benjamin had called the police, and they were on their way. But Griff couldn't risk any of his team leaving Bethany and Ada right now. He felt confident that that was exactly what these guys wanted. To draw them away.

He couldn't let that happen.

Finally, they reached the cottage. Griff ushered Bethany and Ada back inside and instructed Dez and Benjamin to stay with them.

"You're going out there?" Dez's voice sounded tinged with surprise.

"I want to talk to these guys," Griff said. "I need to know what they're up to."

"Isn't that obvious?" Benjamin asked. "They want your family."

Hearing him say the words caused more adrenaline to pump through Griff. "I want to be there when the police come and capture them."

"You don't really think they're going to let that happen, do you?" Dez asked.

"No, but I don't want them to think we're just going to run away either."

Grabbing his gun, Griff stepped outside. As he did, his phone rang.

It was Colton.

If he was calling, there was probably a good reason.

Still on guard, Griff put the phone to his ear. "What's going on?"

"Brian is awake, like I told you," Colton started. "But we think someone is watching him. Elise and I are going to stay here to keep an eye on him. I just wanted to let you know."

That didn't surprise Griff. Brian was probably supposed to die in that accident. When he didn't, someone had come back to finish him off.

"Thanks for the update," Griff said.

By the time Griff stepped over the sand dune, the men were nowhere to be seen. The beach was empty, almost as if nothing had ever happened.

Disappointment bit deep. They'd gotten away. Again.

But these guys were sending the message loud and clear. Nothing was going to stop them. Nothing at all.

BETHANY WATCHED as Griff stepped back inside, and she held her breath, waiting to hear what happened.

"They're gone," Griff announced, a scowl on his face.

She'd expected his words but hoped for something different. But if those men were gone from the beach, where were they now? What were they planning next? Were they preparing for another attack?

None of those questions settled well with her.

Ada continued to fuss in her arms. She'd given her daughter some water and crackers, but it was obvious she was sleepy.

CJ looked up from cleaning out one of the

kitchen cabinets. "If she needs to lie down, you can use my room."

"I think I will try that." If Bethany could get her daughter to take a nap, maybe Bethany would also be able to think more clearly. Her head felt like it might explode right now.

In CJ's room, Bethany lay down next to Ada and rubbed her daughter's back, murmuring soothing words and singing lullabies. Finally, fifteen minutes later, Ada's breathing evened out and sleep found her.

Bethany lay there a moment, trying to clear her head before returning to face reality. As she did, she picked up her phone.

Before she turned it on, she prayed there wouldn't be any more messages that caused her blood to spike. No more videos of her parents' house.

She would never forgive herself if something happened to her parents because of her. Her parents were wonderful people who had given their lives to serving the community and the church. They didn't deserve to be pulled into something like this.

Then again, neither did Ada.

Thankfully, Bethany saw no new mysterious text

messages. Instead, she checked her email one more time.

There was another email from her boss.

She read the words. *I've gotten several questions about the document I sent you all to sign via email earlier today. I want to assure everyone that I did send it, and I do require your signatures on this new document so that we can be HR compliant. I need this document to be signed by the end of the day today. Thank you all for your understanding, John.*

Her heart pounded in her ears. This wasn't what he'd told her earlier. Had something changed?

She'd gotten phishing emails before. Scams popped up all the time. But the fact that this one sounded so personal and professional set off all kinds of alarms in her head.

Eager to dispel her doubts, she dialed John's number again. Her boss answered on the first ring.

"Did you just send out a follow-up email?" Bethany asked, keeping her voice low.

"Follow-up email? No, I told you I didn't send the first one."

"I just got a new one that's supposedly from you. It assures everybody that you did indeed send the first one and that the document needs to be signed by the end of the day. Do you know what's going on?"

"The IT guys couldn't find anything, so we're not really sure how these emails are being sent from my account. They said our firewall is one of the best."

"I don't know either, but it's concerning."

"It is. I'll make sure everyone gets the message not to sign. I don't know what's going on here, but until we do, I'll be cautious."

"Good idea. I just wanted to let you know."

With Ada snoozing, Bethany crept from the room and found Griff in the living room area. He paced by the door, still looking as ticked off as he did earlier. These guys were obviously getting under his skin.

"Did the police find those men?" Bethany asked, anxious for an update.

Griff shook his head. "No, they were long gone. They had it all timed just right."

Disappointment bit deep. "How did they even know we were going to leave the house?"

"They probably didn't. My guess is that they were waiting to see what our next move was and then they played off of that."

It was like these guys had nothing better to do than to make Bethany and Griff miserable. They were putting some time and energy into it, and that bothered Bethany. Why would they do that unless they had something big planned?

A shiver captured her muscles.

Bethany sighed and looked around, trying to concentrate on the knowns instead of the unknowns. "Where is everyone?"

"Benjamin is outside. Colton and Elise are in Raleigh. Cassidy and Ty are up in Virginia Beach."

"And Dez?"

"Apparently, Cassidy found someone up on Hatteras who used to work for NASA. He's looking at the drone for us. Dez took it up to him."

Bethany crossed her arms as a cold chill washed over her. One more thought lingered in her head, but she knew how her words might sound.

Still, her question was worth asking.

She cleared her throat. "I know this is going to sound crazy, but what's the chance that this email that was sent to me through my job is somehow connected with all of this?"

A knot formed between Griff's eyes. "I don't see how this could be connected. You're an associate editor for an engineering magazine. How would that interest the Savages?"

"You're probably right. There's just something about this that's been bugging me."

"There are a lot of unknowns right now."

She couldn't argue that.

"Remind me of something." Griff stopped pacing and paused in front of her. "This job you're working at now . . . it's not the same one you worked at when we were married. Exactly what kind of engineering magazine is this again?"

"It's mostly focused on the energy sector—people who work at energy companies, power plants, and contractors who work the grid."

Griff's face stiffened. "Good to know."

What did that expression mean exactly? Did Bethany really want to know?

CHAPTER TWENTY-THREE

GRIFF'S THOUGHTS RUSHED. The energy sector?

That was a known target for terrorist groups. He'd heard murmurings of such things. In fact, the Savages were known for stealing tantalum out in Africa. The element was used in so many electronic devices.

Without a ready supply of it, the prices for all electronics would be driven up. Many people believe that if someone could control that substance, they could effectively control the tech world.

What if all of the attacks that had happened overseas were just a smokescreen? Even the name of the Savages implied that they were barbarians. But what if that wasn't the case at all?

What if these guys were actually highly sophisticated? What if they were trying to get to Ada and to Bethany's parents as a means of getting to Bethany?

She worked for a publication that focused on engineering in the energy sector. Griff didn't know exactly what the connection might be, but, through her job, she had connections with the people who ran the very power plants that distributed energy throughout the US.

Could Griff be onto something? He didn't know. But it was worth giving some thought to. More puzzle pieces needed to fall in place before he could fully understand.

Griff's phone dinged, and he looked down at the screen. It was a text message.

GUNS ARE AIMED **at the house. No one inside is safe. Go outside with Bethany. Tell anyone, and everyone will die.**

AS GRIFF FINISHED READING the message, he heard a pop and then a groan in the distance. His muscles tightened. What was going on?

He glanced around. Knew that Ada was napping in a bedroom. Saw CJ sitting at the kitchen table reading a book. Spotted Bethany staring out the window, the weight of the world on her shoulders.

This guy messaging him knew that Benjamin was outside. He knew that Griff was with Bethany.

But the last thing Griff wanted to do was to test this guy's limits.

Almost as if the messenger could read his mind, his phone buzzed again. Griff looked down at the screen.

YOU HAVE **twenty seconds to get out the door before I shoot again.**

HIS MUSCLES WOUND EVEN TIGHTER. Shoot again?

Maybe Griff could just go outside alone. Leave Bethany out of this. See what happened.

He stood, knowing that time was ticking away. As he stepped toward the door, apprehension rippled through him.

"Where are you going?" Bethany looked up at him with wide, confused eyes.

"I need to take care of something."

"What?"

He didn't have time to explain things. "I'll be back."

Griff hoped he was telling the truth. He hoped that once he stepped out the door, that it wouldn't be the point of no return. He wasn't ready for things to end like this.

After a brief moment of hesitation, Griff's hand circled the doorknob and he pulled it open. As he stepped into the darkness outside, apprehension filled him. Where was Benjamin?

And the other important question: where was the shooter?

Griff walked to the edge of the screened-in porch and glanced down. His pulse quickened when he saw Benjamin on the ground, holding his side.

Benjamin had been shot.

Griff's gaze shot up, looking for gunmen.

He saw none.

But was that . . .

He glanced at the sky.

A drone buzzed there. An armed drone.

This was worse than he'd thought.

Griff started toward the stairs, desperate to help his friend. But before he could reach Benjamin, his phone buzzed again.

. . .

BRING BETHANY **or I'll shoot again. You have ten seconds. Tell no one what's going on.**

GRIFF'S HEAD POUNDED. He had no doubt that this shooter was serious. He had already put a bullet in Benjamin. His friend needed help.

As much as Griff wanted to leave Bethany out of this, he wasn't sure that he could.

Anxiety churned in his gut, and he hated himself for having to make this choice. But everyone's lives were at stake right now.

He opened the door again and cleared his throat before calling to Bethany. "Could you come here for a minute?"

As soon as the words left his lips, he hated himself for it.

Confusion flooded Bethany's eyes as she stood. "Of course."

Griff glanced at CJ. "Would you mind keeping an eye on Ada for a few minutes?"

CJ glanced down the hall to where Ada was sleeping. "I have to say she's a bit of a handful, but I think I can handle it."

Any other time, that would've gotten a smile out of Griff. But not today. Not knowing what he did.

Bethany stepped onto the screened-in porch, and Griff closed the door.

His heart pounded.

"What's going on?" She looked up at him with those wide eyes that always got to him.

"I'm sorry, Bethany." His voice cracked. There had to be another way . . .

"Sorry?" A knot formed between her eyebrows. "Sorry for what? What's going on, Griff?"

His phone buzzed again.

COME **down the steps and I'll give you more directions. One wrong move and I'll shoot. Everyone in the house will die.**

BETHANY GLANCED at the screen along with him and let out a gasp. "I don't like this, Griff."

"I don't either." Griff took her hand and led her down the stairs, wishing he never had to let go. That he could freeze this moment in time and not move forward. That he could save Bethany from whatever heartache might be waiting for them.

At the bottom of the steps, Bethany spotted

Benjamin. She gasped, and they rushed toward him. He moaned as he lay on the ground.

"He's been shot." Bethany's eyes skimmed the man as trembles claimed her.

Griff frowned as he knelt beside her next to Benjamin.

"The bullet skimmed the side of my abdomen." Benjamin's face scrunched with pain. "But I think I'll be okay."

Griff's phone buzzed.

WALK DOWN THE LANE. **Do it quietly, and no one else will get hurt.**

"I DON'T LIKE THIS, GRIFF." Bethany's voice quivered as she stared at the drone.

Griff rose to his feet, glancing down at Benjamin before saying, "Neither do I. But he's left us with no other choice. I'm sorry I got you involved with this, Bethany."

"It's not your fault, Griff."

He didn't believe that. He knew the truth. He knew that all of this was his fault.

"Benjamin . . ." Griff said.

His friend's face scrunched with pain, but his eyes went to the drone also. "I'll be okay. Dez will be back in a minute. If you don't do what they say, they're going to kill all of us."

His words were true. None of them had much choice here.

Finally, Griff nodded. "Hang on, friend. You're going to be okay."

"God needs to be with us all right now."

Benjamin's words haunted Griff as he and Bethany started down the dark lane. Griff heard the drone following behind. The sound made him keenly aware that if this person wanted to take them out, he could.

Griff lifted prayers. Not for himself. But for Bethany. For Ada.

All he'd ever wanted to do was to protect them. How had it all led to this?

Halfway down the lane, Griff heard a rustling in the brush. As he turned to see what it was, a masked man emerged from the marsh.

Griff pushed Bethany behind him, ready to face this man.

Before he could, a shock rushed through his muscles, taking him to the ground.

A Taser, he realized.

At once, Griff was rendered immobile.

He glanced back at Bethany just in time to see electricity running through her body as well.

A black bag was shoved over his head, and he heard tires on the gravel.

A car must have pulled up.

Someone—probably two people—lifted him. Pushed him into a small space.

The car trunk, he realized.

A moment later, another thump sounded. He felt something—someone—tumble into him. He heard a slight moan.

They'd put Bethany inside also, he realized.

Griff felt powerless to protect her, almost like he was riding a wave that was out of his control. And there was no feeling he hated more.

BETHANY'S HEART RACED. The fear she felt was so vivid that it seemed to crawl across her skin and into her lungs until she could hardly breathe.

Ada...

Her daughter was all she could think about. Would Ada be okay? Now that they had Bethany and Griff, would these men leave her little girl alone? Or was this just a bluff to get Bethany and Griff away from her?

The last thing she wanted was for Ada to grow up without a mother or father. People had done it before, and they'd turned out okay. But it wasn't what Bethany wanted for her daughter. Bethany wanted to be there for Ada as she grew up.

Bethany's eyes were open. She thought they were, at least. The black bag over her head, combined with the dark space of the trunk, made it almost impossible to know for sure. She desperately wanted to see Griff. To talk to him.

She had never seen Griff helpless before. He was always strong, protective. Griff was the one who'd chased down a mugger who'd taken Bethany's purse and put him in a chokehold until the police arrived.

Bethany wanted to reach out to him now, to touch him. She knew it was a bad idea, but she wanted it anyway. She craved human contact, something to let her know that things would be okay.

But would they?

She had no idea. She'd never been in a situation like this before. She would venture to say that most ordinary people hadn't.

She tried to control her breathing, to control her emotions. *Dear God, please help us. Please protect Ada.*

Give us wisdom to know how to handle the situation, whatever it might be.

The Taser still hadn't worn off. Bethany had never felt something so violent before. It claimed her entire body, causing a sharp pain to capture all her muscles.

How long did these effects last? And where were they being taken right now?

Bethany felt the bumps on the road. She heard people murmuring in the front seat.

Were these the Savages? They were known for being brutal. Human life meant nothing to them. That meant they might go to great extremes in order to hurt Bethany and Griff.

A cry tried to escape, but it came out as more of a groan.

At least it was something, right?

She felt Griff twitch beside her. Maybe he was regaining the use of his limbs.

Maybe.

Just as the thought entered her mind, the car pulled to a stop.

Bethany braced herself for what was to come.

CHAPTER TWENTY-FOUR

SOME OF THE feeling returned to Griff's limbs. But not enough to fight back. Not yet, at least.

Where were they?

He would guess that they'd only traveled about five minutes away from Cassidy and Ty's house. There weren't that many places they could get to that fast. Based on the way his body shifted and moved, Griff felt like they were traveling north on the island.

There wasn't much to the north of the island from Ty's house. The church was out this way. Lots of marsh land and eroding shoreline. But not much else.

Except the hotel site. There had been a lot of construction going on there...

So just what were these guys planning? And why did they have to involve Bethany?

His thoughts went back to Ada again. Had someone decided to grab her after he and Bethany had been abducted?

Anger burned through his blood at the thought.

The next moment, the car stopped, the trunk opened, and a whiff of balmy sea air filled the space.

Griff tried to move his arm, but it only came out as a spasm.

There were many things he could defend himself against, but a Taser was not one of them. No doubt these guys had known that.

Griff still couldn't see anything because of the bag over his face.

The two men surrounded him on each side, practically dragging him away from the vehicle. Griff's legs wouldn't work. Instead, they scraped against the ground. He felt the sand at his feet, sand dotted with marsh grass and rocks.

Finally, they stopped. The bag was jerked from his face, and Griff tried to look around, to gather his surroundings.

Before he could, one of the masked men spoke. "We thought you might need a wake-up call."

The feeling began returning to his limbs. As

Griff glanced at Bethany beside him, she still looked immobilized as she lay on the ground. That was going to make any attempt at getting away harder.

"Is that what you call all of this?" Griff scowled at his captors. "A wake-up call?"

"You could say that. Only it hasn't worked. We've always known you're stubborn."

"Why did you bring us here?" Griff glanced around. Saw some construction equipment and building materials. A chain-link fence surrounded the area. They were at the site of the hotel, he realized.

"So you could remember."

"Remember what?"

"That's for you to figure out."

The men reached for him. Griff darted to his feet, ready to tackle his closest assailant. Before he could, they used the Taser again.

He lost all use of his muscles.

One of the men shoved him, and Griff found himself falling. He hit the packed sand below. Pain rippled through him.

The next moment, he heard another thump and a groan.

Bethany.

They'd tossed Bethany in beside him.

Anger burned through his veins.

"You have approximately eight minutes to get out before you're buried alive," the man called from overhead. "Otherwise, not only will you be dead, but so will your daughter."

Ada? Had they grabbed Ada anyway, despite the fact that Griff had followed their instructions?

He couldn't expect evil men to behave honestly. But pain at the thought of what might happen to Bethany and Ada ripped through his heart.

He had to get out of here. Had to save Bethany. Save Ada.

The men disappeared from above him. They were leaving them in here.

Why?

To be buried alive.

To remember.

But what did those things mean?

He wasn't going to have much time to figure it out. Eight minutes to be precise.

Even less time than that, really, because of the effects of the Taser.

Griff studied Bethany a second. Saw the pain and fear on her face.

At least she was okay. She was alive. He needed to keep it that way.

He glanced around. They appeared to be in a huge hole in the sand. If he had to guess, the sides were at least twelve feet high. And they were steep. The walls appeared to be formed from packed sand.

He felt certain this was the hole that had been dug out for the hotel's foundation and septic.

Just as he was trying to comprehend all of that, he heard an engine start.

He glanced over and saw some kind of shaft leading into the space.

Griff's eyes widened when he saw sand begin pouring from it.

This was what the man had meant by being buried alive.

Griff had to gain use of his muscles again.

There was no time to waste.

BETHANY SAW the sand filling the hole, and her pulse quickened with panic. Granules splattered on her, scattering across her face. She squeezed her eyes shut as particles hit them.

This couldn't be happening. She and Griff couldn't be buried alive.

Yet they were.

If Bethany didn't regain use of her limbs soon, the plan these terrorists had set in motion would work.

"Beth... any."

Griff. He was trying to talk. But his voice came out muted and strained.

She squinted, and, through the slit of her eyes, she saw Griff. His eyes were on her, and concern filled them.

He felt responsible. Bethany knew him well enough to know that.

She tried to silently communicate that this wasn't his fault. He always blamed himself for everything. And Bethany understood his dilemma.

He'd grown up in a house where his mom had put all the responsibility on Griff at a young age. He hadn't had an easy upbringing, but Bethany thought he'd turned out pretty well. At least, she thought that until he divorced her.

"Turn..." Griff muttered.

Turn? Griff wanted her to try to roll away from the incoming sand, she realized. Could she do that yet?

She might as well try. She had nothing to lose.

Using all of the energy and strength she could

muster, she tried to rock her body. On the first try, she remained right where she was.

She tried again.

This time, she ended up on her back.

Maybe this would work!

She tried again, and again, and again. Finally, she was able to roll away from the cascade of sand that filled the hole. Griff followed behind.

But she knew their troubles weren't over yet.

The sand poured in too fast.

Bethany tried to move her fingers. Finally, she managed to make a fist.

Good. The effects of the Taser were wearing off.

Her gaze stopped at the dark sky above her. She didn't see the men up there anymore. Were they still watching out of sight?

She didn't know. She would have to worry about that later. They only had eight minutes—probably six now. She assumed that was how long it would take the sand to fill the space.

The granules fell over Griff again. Bethany's eyes widened as she saw the grains cover one side of him. If he wasn't able to sit up soon, the avalanche would consume his face.

Their eyes met again, and millions of unspoken conversations passed in that one glance.

Bethany wasn't sure if they were going to get out of this alive or not.

She wasn't prepared for things to end this way. So much was still unspoken between them. But she could hear the mental timebomb ticking . . . and the final outcome of all this felt overwhelming.

CHAPTER TWENTY-FIVE

GRIFF FELT the sand covering him. Creeping into his ear. Around his neck. Over his shoulder.

He and Bethany didn't have much time.

Even if they did regain total movement, getting out of this gigantic hole was going to be a huge task in itself.

The sand being piped into the space was soft. It would nearly be impossible to use it to climb out. The walls, in the meantime, were steep.

But Griff was nowhere close to giving up yet.

He moved his arm. At least, he tried to.

No... this time, it worked.

He was regaining more movement.

Thank God.

Sand covered part of his chest and one of his

legs. Soon it would reach his mouth and his nose. He couldn't let that happen.

Using all of his strength, Griff turned his head again. He'd bought himself a few more minutes, at least.

Bethany's eyes were wide as she stared at him. There was so much he wanted to say to her. So much.

Why had he been so stupid? Now that he faced death, his choices seemed so obvious. He could've handled things better. But he'd only been trying to look out for the good of Bethany and Ada. Would they ever understand that?

Bethany's arm moved. She flopped it forward until her fingers brushed his. She squeezed, her touch offering a silent reassurance.

A moment of hope fluttered through him.

They were going to get through this. They had no other choice.

Griff mentally counted to three and then pushed himself up.

It worked!

Now he had to get his legs moving.

Sand covered his bottom half. Soon it would cover Bethany.

He reached forward and grabbed her arm again. Using all of his strength, he pulled her up.

She sat up also. As she did, she sputtered.

Good. She was getting any sand out of her mouth.

"Griff..." she gasped.

"Come ... on ..." Griff managed to pull himself to his feet. Once he had his balance, he helped Bethany do the same. They were both still unstable, but at least they were standing.

"How . . . ?" She looked up at him and then looked at the ground above.

That was a good question.

Griff might try to make some foot and hand holes on the side of the wall. But he knew that wouldn't work. The sand wasn't hard enough.

Bethany stepped forward, as if trying to climb up the sand that was being poured into the space.

Instead, she sank into it.

Griff pulled her out before she found herself buried there again.

He had to think, and he had to think quickly before this place became their grave.

BETHANY THOUGHT the worst of her panic was done, but it wasn't. Sure, she was regaining use of her limbs. But their troubles were far from over.

She thought they'd be able to run up the fresh sand being poured into the hole. But the granules were like sugar. Instead of being able to walk on top of it, she just sank down into it.

She turned back to the walls. Griff tried to scale it. But every time he touched it, the surface crumbled. There was no grip.

More panic flooded through her. What were they going to do? They couldn't die like this. Ada needed them.

"Bethany..."

She looked over at Griff. He shook his head, as if letting her know he wasn't sure how they were going to get out of this.

"We can do this," she rasped.

"We can't scale the walls, and we can't climb the sand," he said. "I'm open to more ideas right now."

"There's got to be something."

They both glanced around again, but neither of them seemed to see any solutions.

Instead, they gathered themselves for a moment. This couldn't be it. There had to be something they could do.

But what?

Griff turned toward her, wrinkles forming at the corners of his eyes. "I need to tell you why I left."

"What? Right now?" His timing was awful. They needed to get out of here first. Every minute counted right now.

He grabbed her arms. "Look at me. Please. Just give me thirty seconds."

Bethany pulled her gaze back to his and crossed her arms, trying to quell her anxiety. This was obviously important to him. "Okay..."

"I left you because... I could feel the toll everything was taking on me after Daniel died. I didn't like the person I was becoming. But it was more than that. I only wanted to protect you and Ada. I didn't want the two of you to be caught in the crossfire."

What did that mean? "Go on."

Griff ran a hand over his face, his gaze distraught. "And... I didn't know what to do. Then one day I got home early, and I saw you outside talking to Mason."

"Our neighbor Mason?" What did he have to do with this?

Griff nodded, the lines on his forehead showing the emotional war waging inside him. "You looked so happy. So carefree. I realized that being away from me was the best thing for you."

"Griff..."

"No, it's true. Plus, I was caught up with my work as a Navy SEAL. I feared the wrong people would come looking for me. I just thought... I thought you deserved a chance at happiness. That you deserved a safe life. You couldn't be with me and have those things."

Bethany's surprise turned into anger. Who was he to make that choice for her? All these months of feeling betrayed... and it was for something that could have been avoided.

Her hands fisted at her side. "You don't get to decide what makes me happy, Griff."

"I only want what's best for you and Ada."

"Being away from you was never better." Bethany jabbed her finger into his chest. "Never."

"Bethany..."

"Don't Bethany me." She started to jab him again when he caught her arm. As Griff pulled her close, she pounded on his chest, and unshed tears made their way to the surface.

She didn't want to let Griff hold her. Yet she wanted it more than anything.

And that was a problem.

Just as he stroked her hair a little too tenderly, Bethany backed up. "I can't do this again."

"Do what again?"

"Pretend like we're a family. Pretend like you might love me forever. Pretend—"

"Bethany..."

She shook her head. "It's true. You're right. Ada deserves to be happy. If she gets close to you again only to have you shut us out of your life, then she'll be devastated. I can't do that to her. Or to myself."

Before he could say anything, she turned and walked back to the sand wall.

With any luck, Griff hadn't seen her tears.

CHAPTER TWENTY-SIX

GRIFF GLANCED around one more time, desperate to figure out a solution.

That conversation hadn't gone the way he'd wanted or planned. The timing hadn't been great, but he had to tell Bethany the truth. If they didn't make it out of here, she deserved to know that he'd only been trying to protect her.

Her reaction hadn't surprised him. Griff deserved every insult and jab he'd received.

He only wished he could go back and change things. But it was too late for that. Right now, he had to concentrate on staying alive.

For Ada's sake.

Then he could figure out the rest later.

He glanced around again. There had to be something he was missing.

That's when something on the other side of the space caught his eye.

A root from the tree that had been dug up stuck out of the sand, forming the perfect hand hold.

If they could make it over to it, maybe Griff could grab ahold. Maybe that would give them enough leverage to get out of this grave that had been dug for them.

The challenge would be getting through the soft sand first.

"What are you thinking?" Bethany asked.

She still had that injured look in her eyes. Griff didn't even know what to say, and he knew that right now was not the time to address it. The sand was already up to their knees, and every minute counted.

"We've got to get to that root." Griff pointed across the hole.

"The root?"

"If we can grab hold of it, maybe we can climb out."

"Seems like it's worth a shot. But how do we get to it?"

There was only one way he could think of. "You need to get on my shoulders."

Bethany stared at him. "Really?"

Griff nodded. "Really. I'm going to walk over there and let you take hold of it."

"But you're going to be almost completely covered with sand if you do that."

"I'll be okay," he told her.

"You don't know that." It could be a suicide mission.

"We'll figure something out." His voice left no room for argument.

Bethany stared at him another moment before nodding with resignation. He knelt, and Bethany climbed onto his shoulders. He ignored the memories crushing at him. Memories of playing chicken at poolside parties when they'd been dating. He had so many fond remembrances with this woman. Would she ever fully understand that?

It didn't matter right now.

Griff sucked in a deep breath and began walking toward the root. As he did, he sank deeper into the sand. Each step was like walking through cement. But he couldn't lose his balance and send Bethany toppling into this mess. He *had* to do this.

He needed to rely on all his years of SEAL training. If anyone could do this, Griff knew he could. It was what he had been taught. Survival.

He took smaller steps now, practically shuffling through the soft sand. Bethany ran her hand along the wall beside them, trying to keep her balance.

By the time they reach the root, the sand was up to Griff's chest.

Much farther, and he would be totally immersed. Unable to breathe.

The way the sand filled the space, that might just happen.

He raised his head, trying to keep his mouth as high as possible. "Can you reach it?"

Bethany leaned forward, grabbing at the root.

First try, she missed.

She tried again.

This time, her hands were wrapped around it. "I got it."

"Can you pull yourself up? Use my shoulders if you need to. You can stand on them."

Bethany glanced down at him, and her eyes widened when she saw the sand getting higher and higher. He was going to be completely buried soon.

"Griff..."

"Just do it," he rasped. The sand had almost reached his mouth, his eyes. He knew what was coming.

Bethany's feet hit his shoulders. She stood and

pulled herself up with the root. Using it as leverage, her hands reached the surface.

That was the last thing Griff remembered seeing before sand completely covered him.

BETHANY GASPED for air as she sprawled on the ground. But the moment of regaining her composure lasted only a minute.

"Griff!"

She leaned over the hole and searched for him. He was no longer visible.

Her stomach plummeted. "Griff!"

But he wasn't there. Could he still hear her?

"Griff! Grab my hand!" She lay flat on her stomach and leaned into the pit, careful to keep her balance. She reached forward.

Please, God. Let him hear me. Let him be okay.

She watched and waited.

But she heard nothing.

Tears sprung to her eyes. Had Griff sacrificed his own life to save her? Bethany had known he was that type, but she'd always hoped it wouldn't come down to this.

Bethany was halfway tempted to jump down into

that crater-like space and try to rescue him herself. But she knew that wouldn't work. She would just sink into the sand also.

Had Griff left her because he loved her? She couldn't stop thinking about that conversation. It made no sense.

Yet it did. Because she knew Griff. She knew he would do anything to protect her. She'd have to think more about that later.

There had to be something else that she could do now.

She glanced around.

The truck. The sand in the back of the vehicle filled this place. Bethany had to stop it.

She sprang to her feet and ran over to the vehicle. She ran around the device, looking for some kind of Off button.

Bethany saw nothing.

Instead, she climbed inside. There were so many levers. Which was the right one?

She didn't know. She began pulling them all.

Finally, she glanced back and saw that the bed of the truck had flattened.

Relief shot through her. That should stop the sand. For now.

Bethany could be thankful for that. But she still needed another way.

She glanced around again. What else could she do? There had to be something.

She saw another lever. Figuring she had nothing left to lose, she pulled it. The chute leading into the hole shifted. She stared at it a moment, wondering if that might help her or not.

And then she realized what she could do.

She could use it like a ladder.

Without wasting anymore time, Bethany climbed on top. She prayed that her plan worked and that it didn't end up getting them both killed.

CHAPTER TWENTY-SEVEN

CAREFULLY, Bethany lowered herself down the shaft. She knew that, with one slipup, she would end up in the sand, back in the same predicament she'd started in. But she would do this. She would do it for Griff.

How long had Griff been under that sand now? It felt like thirty minutes, but, in reality, it had probably been only five.

Five minutes? How long had Griff once told her he could hold his breath underwater? It was at least five minutes, wasn't it?

Finally, she reached the bottom of the chute. She sat on the edge.

It ended right where Griff had disappeared.

Careful to leverage herself, Bethany wrapped her legs around the tube and began digging in the sand.

Please, God. Please, God. Please, God. It was all she could pray over and over again.

Finally, her hand hit something.

Was that . . . hair?

Bethany dug deeper, still careful to keep her balance.

A moment later, Griff's face appeared.

His unmoving face.

Her breath caught as worst-case scenarios raced through her mind.

Bethany furiously dug until Griff's face was exposed. But he didn't move. He looked lifeless.

She slapped his cheek. She hit it again and again and again.

"Come on, Griff. Come on!"

But she wasn't sure if his eyes were going to open or not.

Moisture filled her gaze.

He did love her. He loved her enough to sacrifice himself. To sacrifice his happiness.

Bethany just hadn't seen it until now.

She prayed they weren't too late.

GRIFF HAD TRIED to maneuver himself through the sand. He'd held his breath, just like he had been taught to do as a SEAL. Only as a SEAL, he'd been taught to do that underwater. Here, he was doing it in the sand. If he slipped up and inhaled, the substance would fill his nose and mouth and he'd be a goner.

With his eyes closed, he couldn't tell how far he moved, if at all.

After a few moments, Griff paused. Was he going to be able to do this?

He stretched his hands above him. Sand covered them—it was deep. Would he be able to get out?

Despair tried to press into him, but he warded it away.

Something shifted above him.

Please tell me that Bethany has not jumped back in here. Please.

He felt something hit his face . . . he thought.

Were his mouth and nose exposed?

He couldn't chance it.

He couldn't open his eyes or risk taking a breath. Not without knowing if sand still surrounded him.

Then he realized he had no other choice. His lungs were tight. He needed a breath.

He pushed his eyes open. Bethany was there. Staring down at him.

And his face was clear.

Griff sucked in a deep breath, one that ended in a coughing fit.

But he could breathe.

Somehow Bethany had managed to begin digging him out of the sand.

Thank God!

"I'm going to get you out of here." Bethany leaned toward him, her breath shallow with exertion. "I don't know how. But I will."

Gratitude filled his heart. She had every opportunity to run, but she hadn't.

Warrior Princess. Bethany was the original, and Ada was just her mini me.

"Can you take my hand?" Bethany asked.

Griff dragged his arm from the sand and reached for her. Using an impressive amount of strength, Bethany tugged and pulled and tugged and pulled. Finally, Griff was able to grab onto the end of the shaft.

"Back up!" he ordered.

Bethany began scooting upward on the shaft. As she did, Griff pulled himself out of the sand. He drew in a few ragged breaths as he sat there for a moment.

But there was no time to waste. He didn't know where those guys were or what they were planning next. But he knew he had to get Ada. He had to get to her now.

Bethany glanced at him before scrambling back to the top of the chute. She climbed up and onto solid land. Griff followed behind her.

As they both caught their breath, they stood there in front of each other a moment. There was so much that he wanted to say.

But before Griff could get a word out, a step sounded behind him.

Anderson had mentioned something about revenge.

These men had said something about Griff needing to remember something.

There was obviously more here than anyone realized.

If Griff had to guess, this whole incident in the sand pit hadn't been about wanting them dead. It had been about teaching them a lesson.

They were never going to let Bethany die, were they? No, for some reason, she was a target here. The whole setup had been to teach them a lesson.

This was far from being over. The men were

here. They'd probably been here the whole time, just waiting until the sand filled the pit. Then they'd planned on fishing them out. At least, he assumed they'd planned on digging Bethany out.

She was the one they wanted.

Before he could move, another shock went through him.

Something came down over Griff's head, and everything went black again.

CHAPTER TWENTY-EIGHT

BETHANY DIDN'T KNOW how much time had passed. Her captors had Tasered them again.

Best she could tell, they'd put her and Griff on some kind of boat. They'd traveled through the water to a harbor, and then they'd been loaded into the back of a utility van.

After the haze of all that, Bethany's thoughts—and vision—were finally becoming clearer. Her head didn't throb as much, and her tongue didn't feel as much like sandpaper.

Their hoods were gone. She glanced around. Darkness filled the back of the space, barely a hint of light and no windows. She and Griff sat side by side, arm to arm.

Bethany looked at Griff. He was awake—and he

didn't look happy. Based on his expression, he'd been lucid for longer than she had. No doubt, he'd already searched the cargo space of this vehicle.

Without thinking, she ran a hand along his cheek, his jaw. Sand still clung to his skin, his hair looked messy, and his muscles were taut.

Yet he still looked so incredibly tough and handsome—just like the man who'd won her heart all those years ago.

"Are you . . . okay?" Bethany thought for sure that she'd lost Griff earlier—and that thought had done something terrible to her heart. As mad—and hurt—as she'd been, she still loved the man. She'd never stopped.

He grimaced, rubbing the side of his head, and then nodded. "This is about more than Daniel's death."

She stiffened. "What do you mean?"

"These guys have a personal vendetta against me and the rest of the Blackout team."

She shifted toward him. "What do you mean, Griff?"

"I haven't been able to stop thinking about it. These guys . . . they planned all of that back at the hotel construction site for a reason. More than just to torture us or manipulate us."

"I don't understand." Bethany rubbed her forehead, desperate to put the pieces together.

"There was an operation my SEAL team did about two years ago. We didn't know all the details—we didn't need to know them, according to Commander Larson. All we knew was that a terror suspect was hiding out in a compound, and we needed to get him."

"What happened?"

"This man had his family there with him. None of our intel had indicated that. We had to change our plans and abort the mission."

"How does that fit with this?" It made no sense to her that those events were somehow linked to Ada's attempted abduction as well as Griff and Bethany nearly being buried alive.

"Our aborted raid tipped off the wrong people." Griff shook his head. "I heard murmurings that this man's wife was killed, that she was buried alive because of his betrayal."

"So you think..."

"I think this guy wants to make us pay. I don't think you were supposed to die back there, though. I think it was all a lesson in loss and fear and revenge."

"That's ... horrible." Bethany paused. "You have

no idea the name of this guy who might be responsible?"

"No idea. But it's going to be my goal to find out when we get out of here." Griff glanced at her, his eyes softening. "I'm sorry, Bethany."

"This isn't your fault." Her throat felt raw as the words left her lips.

"But it is. I tried so hard to protect you and Ada, but I couldn't do it. I thought if I distanced myself from you both..."

"Oh, Griff..." Grief gripped her heart as Bethany realized what his thought process had been throughout all of this.

It was nothing like she'd assumed.

Because he loved them, Griff had left. The logic was twisted, but, deep down inside, he'd been trying to do the right thing. Bethany still thought it should have been her choice, that he shouldn't have left her out of the loop. But now that she'd had some time to let that sink in, understanding rolled through her.

"I gave my life for the military, and look where it got me?" Griff ran a hand over his face. "Nowhere. Without anyone."

She squeezed his shoulder, desperate to get through to him. "You did great things for our country, Griff. Never forget that. All of that wasn't wasted.

Don't believe that lie, despite some of the things that have happened."

He pushed her hair out of her eye, his gaze softening. "I would do anything for you, you know."

"We're going to need to talk more about that later." More than anything, Bethany wanted to talk now, but she knew they didn't have much time. The van had been stopping and going for the past twenty minutes, if she had to guess. That must mean they were in traffic.

"You promise that we can talk about it later?" Griff asked.

"I promise. We're going to get out of this so we can have that conversation."

"I'm going to hold you to that."

She licked her lips, pushing away the overwhelming feelings that wanted to creep in. "For now, any ideas on how we are going to get out of this?"

"That's what I'm trying to figure out."

Without thinking, she reached down and laced her fingers with his. After a moment of hesitation, Griff squeezed her hand back. Just feeling that connection seemed to give Bethany a surge of strength, of hope.

"I know this is going to sound weird," Bethany

started. "But the one man . . . the leader of the group. His voice sounded familiar."

"Do you know from where?"

Bethany shook her head. "I have no idea. I keep thinking about it, but I'm not sure."

"This could very well be someone you know."

She glanced at him. "Like who?"

"We've explored the idea that it's another SEAL. But we don't know that's true. Is there anyone you can think of who has a connection with you and with the military?"

"I don't know. I mean, I know plenty of military personnel but . . ." Her breath caught.

"What?"

"Cindi's husband . . . I don't want to point the finger at someone who's innocent, but he was asking about where I was. He's a common denominator here."

"What does Cindi do at the magazine?"

"She's a secretary. I . . ." Bethany shook her head. "I don't know."

"We've wondered if there's a connection between all of this and your job."

Bethany stared up at him. "How so?"

"Maybe these guys are targeting the power grid. You'd be the perfect person to help them."

"I'm just an associate editor..."

"But you have connections with all the right people."

She did, didn't she? These guys could have been wanting to get to her this whole time.

The next instant, the van pulled to a stop.

Bethany's heart thrummed against her chest. Whatever these guys were planning, she was about to find out. A surge of panic rushed through her.

What if she didn't get out of this alive? What if this was the end of the road for either her or Griff or both of them?

There was something that she had to get off of her chest just in case. "Griff...?"

He turned to her, his face only inches from hers. "Yes?"

"I thought you should know..." Bethany licked her lips, wondering how to say it. She decided just to get it out there. "I didn't sign all of the divorce papers."

Griff's eyes widened. "What?"

Bethany nodded. "It's true. There were about five places I had to sign. I only signed three."

A knot formed between his eyes. "Why would you do that?"

"Because we always said divorce wasn't in our

vocabulary. It's not what I want for my life. Not signing somehow made me feel like I had a little bit of power in it."

"But my lawyer . . ." Griff shook his head as if trying to process that.

"Your lawyer was horrible. And cheap. You got what you paid for. I doubt he even looked the papers over before he filed them."

"I can't deny that . . . but what does that mean?" Griff's gaze was intense as he searched her eyes for answers.

"I'm not sure. I suppose our marital status could go either way. I mean, we haven't gotten our official divorce papers yet."

"So . . . there's a chance we're still married?"

Bethany shrugged. "I guess."

Moisture filled his eyes. Bethany had only seen Griff cry one other time, and that was when his mother died. Seeing him get emotional right now did something strange to her heart. It made it swell with love and longing.

He reached for her, resting his hand at her neck. "Bethany . . . you're the best thing that ever happened to me. If we don't get out of this alive—"

"We can't talk like that." She touched his lips,

ready to press her fingers into them and silence him if he talked like that again.

"I know that we shouldn't. I do. But there are still just some things that need to be said. I love you, Bethany. I always have, and I always will, and nothing is ever going to change that."

Their gazes locked. Bethany wanted nothing more than to kiss this man, to show him how she felt. She wanted to erase the past year—all the hurt, the tears—and start over again. But maybe, at the end of this, they would come out stronger.

Before she could say anything else, the van door flew open. A masked man grabbed Bethany and jerked her out.

The last thing she heard was Griff yelling "No!"

GRIFF'S PANIC turned into a burst of anger. He grabbed the van door and pulled on it. It was no use—it was locked.

What exactly were those men planning on doing with Bethany? Fury burned inside him at the thought. And what about Ada? Was she okay?

None of this was their fault. Couldn't these men just leave them out of this?

Unless it was like Griff had assumed earlier. Maybe this was more about Bethany than he ever imagined. Maybe this was about revenge, about making Griff pay for the heartache he'd caused during his missions as a SEAL.

In the brief moment the van door had been opened, Griff had caught a quick glimpse of the world outside. They appeared to be parked in front of an office building. By his estimation, they'd probably been on the road for four hours. That was enough time to make it to Virginia Beach.

Were they at Bethany's office? Griff didn't know. He'd never been there to know what it looked like.

The bad feeling continued to brew inside his gut.

He hated feeling helpless. Hated feeling like he was just sitting here and couldn't protect the woman he loved.

Yes, the woman he loved. There was no doubt about that. There never had been.

Hearing that Bethany hadn't signed all of the divorce papers had done something strange to Griff's heart. She'd always been feisty in her own way. Willing to go against the flow when necessary. It had always been one of the things that Griff loved about her.

Knowing that she'd never given up on them ... it

only confirmed that he loved Bethany more than anything.

He tugged at the door again. It was still locked, as he'd expected.

He couldn't just sit here.

He moved around the back of the van again, looking for anything that might help him escape this prison where he was being held. But there appeared to be no way out.

Griff had to do something. Because sitting here helplessly wasn't his MO.

He had to figure out another way out of the situation.

Bethany's and Ada's lives depended on it.

CHAPTER TWENTY-NINE

BETHANY CLOSED her eyes and lifted another prayer. A prayer for peace. The last thing she wanted to do was to leave Ada behind. But Bethany wasn't afraid of death. If this was the way it was all going to end, she needed to accept that. And, above all, she needed to do the right thing—no matter how hard that might be.

She stood in front of the four-story building she worked at every day. It was located in an office park in Virginia Beach. It was the middle of the night right now, and no one else was around.

No one but her, and the three men who currently surrounded her.

She looked at her captors. They all wore masks.

Why were they trying so hard right now to

conceal their identities? When they'd walked down the beach earlier, they hadn't worn masks. Was that because they'd been so far away?

Bethany supposed it didn't matter.

"What do you want from me?" She stared up at the men as they surrounded her, unable to control the defiance in her gaze.

"Do exactly what we tell you, and Griff will live."

There was that voice again. Where had she heard it before? She felt certain that she recognized it.

She remembered what Griff said about someone in the command possibly being part of this. Could this guy be another Navy SEAL? Could he be one of the high-ranking officers who oversaw the team? Or maybe somebody else in the commander's entourage? She'd been around all of them at one point or another.

But she wasn't sure.

"What do you want me to do?" Bethany glanced at the man who appeared to be their leader and waited for his instructions.

"You're going to go inside and install this on your computer." The man pulled a jump drive from his pocket.

She stared at the device, fear slithering through her. "What's on it?"

"It's not important. Once it's finished installing, your job will be done."

What could these guys possibly be planning? Was this some kind of malware?

One of the conferences Bethany had recently attended flashed in her mind. A track there had been about dealing with a terrorist attack on America's power grid.

That's what this was, wasn't it? If these guys could get into the computer systems at the editorial office, it would open a back door to reach their contacts. If anyone at those companies actually clicked on a link that was sent, that could potentially give these guys access to the systems at different power companies.

That had to be it. It was the only thing that made sense.

This had never been about Griff, had it? It had about Bethany the whole time. They wanted to kidnap Ada to use her as leverage to make Bethany do their dirty work. When that didn't work, they began harassing Griff and Bethany.

The bad feeling in her stomach only grew.

"Now, let's get inside and get to work," the man said.

Before Bethany could object, he took her arm.

His grip squeezed into her muscles so tightly she was sure to have a bruise. But if Bethany came away from this with only a bruise, she would consider herself fortunate.

The man led her to the door, and Bethany realized she had a quick decision to make.

GRIFF HAD to think of a way to break out of this van.

He felt along the edge of the vehicle again, trying to find something that he might be able to use. At surface level, there was nothing.

But what if . . . ?

He lifted the carpet and found the area where the spare tire was stored. He felt around until his fingers hit metal. He gripped the tool there and held it up: a lug wrench. He could potentially use this as a weapon.

His thoughts raced.

How about Ada? Was she okay? These guys had Griff and Bethany. Maybe that meant they didn't need his daughter anymore. He didn't know, and he didn't like not knowing.

He needed to see if there was anything else he

could use to get out right now. As he felt around the spare tire, he found something else.

A flare.

The kind that could be used on the side of the road during a breakdown. He stared at it for a moment. How could he use this?

There was only one idea that came to his mind. But it would be risky. And, if it backfired, Griff would practically be setting a death trap for himself.

He needed to think this through. And he didn't have much time.

CHAPTER THIRTY

CASSIDY SAT IN HER CAR, Ty by her side, and tried Griff's number, but he didn't answer. Sitting back in her seat, she tried to figure out who was next on her list of people to call. She decided to try Dez. She wanted an update on what was going on back in Lantern Beach—and she'd also learned a couple things herself.

Dez answered on the first ring.

"Cassidy." Based on the sound of Dez's voice, something was wrong.

"What's happening?" She got right to the point. With everything that had happened lately, there was no time to waste.

"Somebody flew a weaponized drone over the house and shot Benjamin. They abducted Griff and

Bethany also. We've been looking for them but haven't located them yet."

"A weaponized drone?" Cassidy sucked in a breath, horrified at the thought of it all. She hit a button, putting the phone on speaker so Ty could hear everything also. "What else? How's Ada?"

"She's fine. She was napping and CJ was watching her when all of this happened. The men broke into the house after they grabbed Griff and Bethany, but CJ and Ada hid in the cabinet beneath the sink. It worked. The guys didn't find them."

"You called my guys and told them? And you told Mac also?" Mac was a former police chief, and he was always ready to step in when Cassidy needed a hand. She would trust him any day with her job.

"I've talked to all of them, and we've been out searching the island. I can't imagine that they got too far. But wherever they are, we haven't been able to locate them yet."

Her heart pounded in her ears at the thought. "How is Benjamin doing?"

"He appears to be doing okay, but he's down at the clinic right now. It was just a surface wound."

"I wish I was there to help."

Ty reached over and squeezed her hand, reassuring her that everything would be okay.

"We know you would be jumping in with both feet if you were here." Dez paused. "Were you able to find out anything?"

"With the help of local police, I found the guy from Ada's daycare," Cassidy started. "Someone paid him big bucks to take those pictures and to plant that knife. He was in serious debt, which is why he did it. But we don't believe he's affiliated with the Savages otherwise."

"How about Jason?"

"He clammed up." Cassidy remembered her meeting with him. It had been uneventful, and the man had been smug, which had made her blood boil. But it wasn't all bad news. "I did find out from the lab that there was a DNA match on the blood. It belongs to someone named Richard Davis."

"Who is Richard Davis?" Dez asked.

"Richard worked for an energy broker in western North Carolina. He was believed to have been killed in a random mugging about two months ago."

"What does he have to do with all of this?" Confusion tinged his voice.

"That's what we're trying to figure out."

"Wait . . ." Excitement rose in Dez's voice. "Bethany works for an engineering magazine, and she received a suspicious email. Griff told me he wondered if there might be some type of connection between all of this and Bethany's job."

Cassidy let his words wash over her. "What do you mean exactly?"

"I'm talking about terrorists who are interested in the power grid here in the United States. There's been chatter about it for years. Based on some previous things that have happened, some experts believe that one way they'll target the power grid is by trying to find a back door into those computer systems. An engineering magazine that goes out to all of the industry professionals would be worth looking into."

"The magazine she works for is based here in Virginia Beach, correct?"

"That's right."

Cassidy started her car. It looked like she wouldn't be heading home after all. She needed to go check out Bethany's workplace instead.

CHAPTER THIRTY-ONE

BETHANY'S HANDS trembled as she punched in the code for her building. No doubt when all of this was over, the police or the FBI would realize that she'd come to the office after hours. All of this would be traced back to her.

No doubt that was part of these guys' plan also.

Her mind continued to race. Continued to think about the conference she'd attended. Continued to think about all the consequences that had been mentioned that would happen if the terrorists were able to attack the sources of energy here in the country.

It would cause panic. Be a means of intimidation.

On a larger scale, an attack on the electrical grid

could cripple the US economy. Could lead to greater things like targeting nuclear power.

One guard had stayed back by the van near Griff. The two others escorted Bethany inside. One of them kept a gun to her side, making it clear that any wrong move would result in injury.

Yes, injury. They wouldn't kill her, not until she had done their dirty work for them.

No doubt they could do this themselves. However, the network here at the company was top-notch with its firewalls. Nobody would be able to get into Bethany's computer without her password and an intricate verification system. It had been set up that way on purpose.

She supposed these guys had assumed they'd grabbed the weak link. Bethany didn't like being thought of as a weak link. She couldn't let herself become collateral either. Or Griff.

When she'd seen the tears well in his eyes, Bethany had known without a doubt that she wanted the two of them to work things out. She'd never wanted to get divorced from him in the first place.

Now hearing about the real reasons why Griff had left her . . . That only confirmed that they needed to give their marriage another chance. Ada deserved it.

Griff had only been trying to look out for her and Ada, especially in light of what happened to Daniel.

Her stomach clenched. Daniel. Poor Elise.

To be told that her husband had died in a training exercise, only to have the truth revealed that a terrorist had killed him during a black ops mission? Though Elise had to be proud of her husband's service, it also had to be difficult to know that her husband had been killed by the enemy.

These guys didn't play well with others.

Bethany walked up the stairs to her third-floor office. Her hands still trembled as she entered the code to get inside. The light turned green, and she twisted the door handle.

They were in.

With the men beside her, Bethany stepped into the space. Darkness hung around her, making the place feel eerie.

She didn't bother to turn on any of the lights in the main room. Instead, she walked toward her office, which was located across the room. She could get there with her eyes closed.

Bethany stepped inside the familiar space and

went to her desk. One of the gunmen—the one whose voice she thought she recognized—remained beside her while the other guy stood lookout near the door.

As she stared at her computer, the man held the jump drive. Bethany's gaze drifted to the picture of her and Ada on her desk. It had been taken on Ada's birthday. Balloons and streamers hung in the background, and they both wore colorful hats.

Ada...

Bethany's heart ached as she looked at the picture.

"Just do it," the man growled beside her.

She snapped back to reality and turned her attention back to the computer. "I'm trying. Your gun isn't helping."

"I don't want you to try anything."

"I am capable of many things, but taking down an armed man isn't at the top of my list of talents."

Bethany could have been certain she heard him laugh.

The feeling returned to her again. That laugh... it had sounded so familiar.

Where had she heard it before? Her mind raced through all the other members of the SEAL platoon.

Only Griff and the three other men of Blackout

had decided to leave the military after the incident with Daniel. There were still plenty of other guys on their SEAL team. Some were still on the team, and some had been shifted over to other teams. Could this man be one of them?

What about Anderson Bryant? He had fed Griff information. But what if he was working for the other side?

Nothing made sense.

Bethany tried to turn on her computer but nothing happened.

"Don't play games with me," the man hissed. "Let's get this over with."

"I'm not playing games. My computer's not coming on."

He cocked the gun and place it against her neck. "Then fix it. Now."

GRIFF LIFTED a quick prayer before lighting the flare. It sparked to life.

He pulled his shirt over his mouth, trying to protect his lungs as long as possible as smoke filled the space.

Then he dropped the flare next to the back door.

With any luck, smoke would begin to creep out the cracks. If his plan went accordingly, the guard would wonder what was going on and open the door.

That was when Griff could make his next move.

However, if the guard didn't take the bait, Griff was in trouble.

Knowing he had no time to waste, Griff began pounding at the door and yelling for help.

Finally, he heard a creak. Then the door opened.

Griff smashed the wrench into the man's head. The man dropped to the ground.

Griff dragged him into the back of the van and took his gun, tucking it into his waistband.

After tossing out the flare, Griff slammed the door, locking the man in the cargo area. Now he needed to figure out how to get inside this building and help Bethany.

He jogged to the front door and pulled on it. It didn't budge, just as he had expected. The glass was tempered and would be hard to break through. There was a keypad, but it would take him too long to try to figure out the code.

There was only one thing he could think to do.

He rushed back to the van. The keys were still in the ignition.

Perfect.

He was going to use this vehicle as a battering ram.

CHAPTER THIRTY-TWO

BETHANY FELT along the edge of the computer, trying to figure out what was going on. She touched the back and realized one of the cables had come unplugged. It often became loose, and she'd requested that it be replaced several times.

At least, she could fix this.

Quickly, she inserted the cord back into its port. A few minutes later, her computer booted up. She let out a sigh of relief.

"Now what do you want me to do?" Bethany looked up at the man.

He showed her the jump drive again. "It's easy. Just insert this, and your job will be done."

"And then what?"

"And then you and Griff can go on your happy way."

"You don't really think I believe that, do you?" Bethany was buying herself some time. But she didn't know what else to do. She couldn't insert this jump drive.

"Are you saying I don't keep my promises?"

"How do I know you?" Bethany stared at him, trying to place the man.

His eyes narrowed. "You're talking too much. Put the jump drive in."

"I'm waiting for the screen to come up so I can enter my passcode."

"You better hope this doesn't take much longer."

She glanced back at the screen. "Someone's going to catch you, you know."

"By the time they catch us, our job will already be done."

"I have to say, I'm impressed. You guys come across like you're brutes. But, in truth, you probably have a whole army of cyber geniuses behind you, don't you? It's like the ultimate sleight-of-hand trick."

Bethany couldn't be sure, but it almost looked like the man smiled beneath that mask.

"The fact that you're catching on to these things

isn't doing much for your chances of survival," he growled.

She shivered. But she knew, at this point, that this man had no intention of letting her walk away.

Finally, the screen came up. Bethany positioned her fingers over the keyboard so she could enter her passcode.

As she paused, she reminded herself that if she put that jump drive in, she could be putting entire parts of the country at risk. But if she didn't, Griff and Ada were at risk.

She knew she should choose the greater good. She did.

But Bethany didn't know if she would really be able to do that or not. Her gaze went to her daughter's picture again.

Ada was just an innocent little girl. She didn't deserve any of this. She needed more birthdays. To live more life.

Sweat formed on Bethany's brow. She didn't know what to do. She didn't know what the right thing was. Or, even if she did know the right thing, she didn't know if she was capable of carrying it out.

"Put your code in," the man said.

With trembling hands, Bethany typed in her password.

One step at a time, she reminded herself. She'd done this now—but not all was lost. Not yet.

The man handed her the jump drive, and Bethany stared at it a minute.

What should she do?

Her precious little girl's face washed through her mind. She remembered the sweet feeling of those little arms around her. She remembered that honey-scented hair. She remembered the sweet way Ada said, "I love you, Mommy."

How could Bethany choose to have her daughter die over this? A lump formed in her throat.

"Put it in," the man growled.

"I can't do this," she said.

"Just do it," the man said.

"But—"

Before the conversation could continue, a loud crash sounded downstairs.

Bethany's heart rate quickened. What was happening?

The man beside her glanced at the guard at the door. "What was that? Go check it out. Now!"

GRIFF FELT his neck stiffen at the impact of

crashing through the doors. He'd have to worry about that later. For now, he climbed from the van, gun in hand, and dashed around the corner.

If things went as planned, one of the guards would be coming down the steps any minute now.

Before Griff had driven through the entry, he'd seen a dim light on the third floor. That must be where Bethany was. That's where he was going to go as soon as he took the guard out.

He gripped his gun as he waited. Finally, he heard footsteps coming down the steps.

He listened as they got closer and closer.

Finally, when it sounded as if the person had reached the bottom, Griff turned. Without hesitation, Griff pulled the trigger. The bullet hit the man in the shoulder, and he let out a yelp. The guard's gun dropped from his hand.

Griff grabbed it and stuck it in his waistband. As the man groaned, Griff pulled him toward a closet. He stashed the man inside and pulled a table in front of the door. That should keep this guy out of commission for a little while, at least.

Griff rushed up the steps. He needed to plan this next move carefully. No doubt the man upstairs with Bethany—the leader—had heard the van hit the building. He'd heard the gunshot.

Either Griff had gotten shot or this man's foot soldier had.

But Griff couldn't do anything that would hurt Bethany or put her in harm's way. She was already in enough danger as it was.

When he reached the third floor, he noticed that all the lights were still off. Good. The darkness would conceal him.

Griff stepped into the doorway and remained against the wall, trying to stay out of sight.

He scanned everything around him. On the other side of the large office space was a glowing light that seemed to be coming from a computer.

As he looked more closely, he saw Bethany sitting behind it. Then he saw the masked man with her, holding a gun to her neck.

Griff would need to plan his next move very carefully.

CHAPTER THIRTY-THREE

BETHANY CONTINUED to stare at the jump drive in her hand. Her decision made nausea churn in her stomach. Either way, it seemed like a no-win situation. What was she going to do?

That was when she heard the gunshot downstairs. Her breath caught.

What was going on? Had Griff been shot?

A cry escaped from her lips at the thought of it.

"That's right," the man beside her growled. "Most likely, that was Griff. You know if we shot him that we're not going to hesitate to shoot your daughter either. You might as well go ahead and get this over with."

Bethany narrowed her eyes. "You're despicable."

"That's the only way to get things done. Now do it."

She squeezed the jump drive. She couldn't do this. She couldn't be part of a large-scale terrorist attack on her own country. It just wasn't right.

Maybe she could think of another way to save Ada. But how would she do that if she didn't get out of here alive?

The pressure continued to mount inside Bethany until she felt like she couldn't breathe. Sweat scattered across her skin. Her hands trembled.

The next instant, the masked man grabbed the jump drive from her. He jammed it into her computer himself.

He shoved her chair away, just in case Bethany considered pulling it out before it fully loaded. Bethany could hardly breathe as she watched the computer begin processing the information.

"There. Was that that hard? Now we just need to wait."

Bethany's throat tightened. She looked at the screen. Five percent had already been installed. It was going faster than she would like.

"What is it downloading?" she asked.

"A way for us to get into your servers. With a few little clicks on our part, we'll be able to get into the computers for all the various people who read your magazine. If we can get into their computers, we can take over the power system."

"You make it sound too easy."

"We've been testing this out for years. It's going to work."

"You're the one who sent the email from my boss's computer, didn't you?" She tried to put the pieces together.

Something flickered in his gaze. "As a matter of fact, yes, we were. That was just a test. When it didn't work, we realized we had to take more drastic measures."

"Why did you try to take Ada? And Elise? Wasn't it me you wanted all along?"

"Leverage, my dear. Leverage. But now we're impatient. We need this done. Now."

Bethany remembered the crash downstairs. Maybe someone nearby heard it. A security guard monitored these parking lots in the evenings. Maybe he had seen it and would report it to authorities. Bethany had to stay positive.

"I've always admired you, you know. If circumstances had been different..."

Bethany looked up at the man who held a gun to

her and narrowed her eyes. "I don't even want to know what that means."

"It means that you are an extraordinary woman, Bethany McIntyre."

"I'd say thanks, but I can't." She practically spit the words out.

Just then, a bullet blew through the air. It hit the man beside her in the chest. He let out a gasp and clutched his chest.

But the gun remained in his hand.

He grabbed Bethany and put an arm around her neck. The gun went to her head, even as blood seeped from his wound.

"Whoever you are, put down your weapon before I kill her," the man said.

Bethany heard the man gasping behind her. Had the bullet hit his lung? He wouldn't have much more time. If she could just stall . . .

But if she delayed too long, the program would continue to load.

Griff stepped from the shadows.

Bethany's heart filled with relief. He was alive! Thank goodness.

But they were far from being done with this. The gun at her temple made that entirely clear.

"Let her go," Griff growled.

"I'm the one calling the shots here," the man holding her rasped.

"Let her go," Griff repeated.

"Put down your weapon or I'll put a bullet through her head." The man's voice continued to weaken, and his grip around Bethany seemed to be loosening.

Bethany glanced at the computer screen. Seventy-five percent already.

This wasn't good.

She had to do something.

Before she could second-guess herself, she rammed her elbow into the man's chest—right in the area where the bullet had hit him. He let out a groan, and his grip on her loosened even more.

Quickly, she turned and grabbed the gun from him. She shoved him out of the way, and he toppled to the ground. With the gun aimed at him, Bethany reached forward and pulled the jump drive from the computer.

Eighty-one percent. She wanted to close her eyes with relief, but she had no chance for that. The download had been stopped. That was all that mattered.

Griff took the gun from her hand.

"You okay?" he asked, keeping one eye on the man.

Bethany nodded, but shivers wracked her body.

"You did good," he said. "Real good."

Bethany collapsed in the chair, her legs no longer able to hold her up.

Griff kept the gun on the man as he moaned on the floor. Sirens sounded outside. Someone must have called the police. Thank goodness.

"Let's see who the man behind the mask is now." Griff reached forward.

Bethany held her breath as she waited to see who he was.

GRIFF JERKED the man's mask off and blinked at the face he saw. "Mason?"

The man shook his head briefly before his face twisted in pain again. "This isn't the end, you know. The two of you aren't going to ruin our plan."

Bethany stared at her neighbor in disbelief. "I can't believe you were behind this."

"The two of you have been a target for a long time, you just didn't know it. I moved in next door to keep an eye on you. When you got the job with this engineering magazine, things just fell into place. We realized that you would be the perfect person to help us enact our plan."

Disgust roiled in Griff's stomach. The lengths these men would go to in order to destroy this country were astounding and desperate. How could someone hold this much hate in them?

"Who else are you working with?" Griff demanded, still holding the gun at the man.

"You'll have to figure that out on your own." Even in his injured state, Mason still sounded smug.

"I know you're working with someone else." Griff leaned down, pressing the gun into Mason's chest. "Who is it?"

"I'd rather kill myself than tell you any more information."

"Maybe we can get that information out of him," a new voice said.

Griff glanced back and saw Cassidy and Ty standing in the doorway, along with officers from Virginia Beach. They flooded into the room.

"How's Ada?" Bethany rushed.

"She's fine."

"Benjamin?" Griff added.

"He's also fine." Cassidy frowned. "How are the two of you?"

"We've been better." Griff glanced at Cassidy. "But we've also been a lot worse."

Bethany flashed him a smile, understanding the implications of what he was saying.

Paramedics rushed in, and officials took over the scene.

What a day this had turned out to be.

CHAPTER THIRTY-FOUR

THE REST of the night was a blur. Not only had the local police come, but the FBI had also shown up. Griff and Bethany had given their statements multiple times. They remained at the office building while law enforcement collected evidence.

Finally, around five a.m., Bethany and Griff were released, as long as they promised to be available if more questions arose.

Griff couldn't wait for a moment alone with Bethany. More than anything, they needed to talk. To *really* talk.

Their gazes met across the room, and Griff nodded to the door. They met there, and he put his hand on the small of Bethany's back to lead her into the hallway.

As soon as they were away from any watching eyes and listening ears, Griff pulled her into a long hug. The kind of hug he'd been wanting to give her as soon as they had reconnected. The kind that had no restraint.

Bethany folded into his embrace. They didn't have to say anything to have hours' worth of silent conversations about their relationship, about what had just happened.

He'd almost lost Bethany today. He couldn't handle that thought. He never wanted to lose her again.

They stepped back from each other, and their gazes met.

"Griff . . . there's so much I want to say." Bethany pressed her lips together.

"Me too." He pulled her toward him and pressed a tender kiss on her forehead. How did he even begin to try to make things right?

"I'm sorry to interrupt," a voice said behind them.

They turned and saw Cassidy standing there with an apologetic smile on her face. Griff left an arm around Bethany as they faced her.

"There are a few things that I thought you might want to know," Cassidy said. "First of all, the knife that was found in Ada's bag was used by Jason Perkins. The blood found on it matched someone named Richard Davis. He worked for an energy broker out in western North Carolina, and he was killed in a supposedly random mugging. Now that we know about the tie to the power grid, however, we know that there was more to that story."

"I wonder how the knife got into the bag," Bethany said.

"Sal from the daycare did it. The Savages paid him off to keep an eye on you."

"What about the drone?" Griff asked. "Have you heard any updates on that?"

"Our contact is still investigating it, but the technology used is apparently amazing. This has given us insight as to what the Savages are planning. Maybe we can head them off at the pass."

"Thanks for the updates," Bethany said.

Cassidy glanced back. "I need to stick around for a couple more hours to wrap this up. However, if you guys want to use my car, you're welcome to go somewhere and get cleaned up. We'd be happy to give you a ride back to Lantern Beach after that."

Griff and Bethany exchanged a look.

"That sounds great," Griff said.

Maybe this was over. Finally over.

AFTER BETHANY GOT out of the shower back at her condo and finished drying her hair, she wandered out into her living room and saw that Griff was already seated on the couch.

Thankfully, she'd found some of his extra clothes not too long ago and had saved them in a box in the corner of her closet. He'd donned some of those now.

As soon as she stepped out, Griff rose from his seat and met her halfway. Tension crackled between them.

"Would you like some water?" Bethany licked her lips, which were suddenly feeling dry.

"I could take some water."

She felt an unusual rush of nerves as she went into the kitchen and poured him a glass. After she handed it to him, she boosted herself up onto the kitchen counter. Griff stood in front of her, his water glass untouched.

Bethany draped her hands on his shoulders as he stepped closer. They had a lot to talk about.

But, before they could start, something invisible seemed to pull them together. Bethany's gaze went to his lips. They leaned closer, close enough that she could feel Griff's breath on her cheek.

Then his lips claimed hers.

Passion that had been building between them exploded in the moment. Bethany had forgotten just how good Griff's lips felt against hers. Tugging. Exploring. Expressing.

As they pulled apart, they still clung together, almost as if neither of them wanted to ever let go. Bethany knew *she* didn't.

"We really need to talk." Bethany's voice sounded raw, even to her own ears.

"Yes, we do."

"I want you to be back in my life," she said.

"I really want to be back in your and Ada's lives also."

"But we need to do it right. We shouldn't rush into anything. I can't handle being hurt again." She had to be smart about this, even if everything in her wanted to blindly jump in with both feet. They clearly still had issues to work through.

"I never wanted to hurt you. And I'm so sorry that I did." Griff caressed her jaw with his thumb.

Bethany closed her eyes, relishing his touch. She craved his closeness.

She'd been slow to admit it, but she'd missed

Griff so badly. Being away from him made her feel like a part of herself was missing.

Bethany absently rubbed her hand against his chest as she tried to slow her thoughts. "So we take this slow. And we set boundaries. We should be responsible."

"I'll do whatever you want me to." Griff's voice sounded raspy as he dipped his head toward hers.

Bethany smiled. "Good. Right now, I want you to kiss me again."

His grin reflected hers. "I can do that."

EPILOGUE

ONE WEEK LATER

AS BENJAMIN and CJ built a sandcastle with Ada, Griff and Bethany walked along the shoreline. It was the perfect spring day—not too hot and not too cold. With nothing else on their agenda, the gang had decided to have a fun day together on the shore.

Bethany wasn't complaining.

Her fingers laced with Griff's as they walked. There were fewer things as sweet as the feeling of walking with him hand in hand.

Her husband.

The divorce papers had been thrown out, and Bethany and Griff were moving full speed ahead with their reconciliation. Elise was doing some counseling with them, and, so far, it was going exceedingly well.

A burst of warmth exploded inside Bethany every time she thought about it. In all the scenarios that had played out in her mind, this happy ending hadn't been one of them. But she was so glad it was reality.

Ada had been overjoyed as well. She couldn't get enough of her daddy.

The two of them were staying here in Lantern Beach for a while. Bethany's boss was letting her work from home. The change allowed her and Griff the chance to reconnect.

Griff paused on the shore and turned to her, brushing a hair from her eyes. His gaze was smoky and intense as he looked at her.

"I love you, Bethany."

She stood on her tiptoes and planted a quick kiss on his lips. "I love you too, Griff."

"You know what else I love?"

"What's that?"

"Throwing you in the water!"

Before Bethany realized what was happening, Griff flung her over his shoulder and began turning her in circles. She let out a scream and beat on his back, but he just laughed.

Finally, he ran into the water and lowered Bethany, catching her in his arms before she hit the ocean.

"Don't do it," she cautioned when she saw the mischief still dancing in his eyes.

He raised his eyebrows. "Or else what?"

"I'll make you pay."

"I like the sound of that."

"Griff . . ." she warned, her voice trailing with laughter.

"Okay," he said. "You win. I won't drop you in."

He gently lowered her to her feet instead.

"Thank you," Bethany said.

But as they turned to head back to shore, she jumped on his back, effectively pushing him in the ocean.

He could have stopped himself if he wanted to. She knew that. But instead, they both went under and came up laughing.

Griff's arms wrapped around her waist, and he stared into her eyes. "I feel like the luckiest guy on earth."

"You are pretty lucky," Bethany told him.

A grin spread across his face before he lowered his lips to hers. The kiss only lasted a minute when someone called their names.

"Mommy! Daddy!" Ada came running toward

them and managed to somehow jump into both of their arms at once. "Look at my castle."

Bethany glanced over to CJ and Benjamin. They both stood wiping the sand from their legs before presenting the castle with a flourish.

"It's so nice," Griff said. "You did this yourself?"

"Benny and CJ helped."

Griff flashed a smile at them. "They're great helpers, huh?"

"Yes, Daddy."

Griff leaned closer to Benjamin and whispered, "She has you under her thumb."

"Who?" A tinge of defensiveness rose in his voice.

"Ada, of course. Who did you think I was talking about?"

Benjamin let out a laugh. "No one has me under their thumb."

Benjamin crossed his arms, and his gaze drifted to CJ.

Bethany wondered if there was something between the two of them, but she knew better than to bring it up.

Instead, she turned her attention to the applause that sounded in the distance.

"What's going on over there?" Bethany asked,

glancing back at their group of friends as they gathered on the beach.

Griff followed her gaze. "Let's go find out."

They all walked toward their friends and got there just in time to see Colton slide a ring onto Elise's finger.

They were engaged.

Bethany smiled. She was so happy for her friends. They deserved a chance at love.

As everyone congratulated Colton and Elise, Bethany and Griff stood back.

"By the way, did you ever figure out who sent CJ that text, telling her to come to the house at just the right time so she was able to save Elise and Ada?" Bethany asked.

Griff shook his head. "We didn't. Strange, huh?"

"It doesn't make sense. Maybe we'll figure out the answer eventually."

"Maybe. I also need to figure out who was involved with that raid—the one where the man's wife was buried alive," Griff said. "I have a strange feeling he might have something to do with all of this."

"It's strange how everything we do has a ripple effect, isn't it? One decision affects another, which affects another."

"Then you make another choice, and the process starts over—only this one will have positive effects." Griff cast a tender smile at Bethany.

"Yes, it will."

Bethany knew this wasn't all over. Not yet. But she was going to enjoy this moment while it lasted.

As Ada pulled them both into a hug, Bethany and Griff planted kisses on her cheeks. She giggled happily.

The road leading here had been rough and broken, but Bethany was so glad the path had led the three of them back together again.

COMING NEXT: RISING TIDE

A FORMER SEAL UNDER SCRUTINY

Benjamin James knows there's a traitor within his former command. The rest of his team might even think it's him. As danger closes in, he must clear himself and stop a deadly plot by a dangerous terrorist group.

A WOMAN CAUGHT IN THE CROSSFIRE

All CJ Compton wanted was a new start after her career ended under suspicion. Working as the house manager for private security group Blackout seems perfect. But there's more trouble here than what she left behind.

A BATTLE TO THE END

As the tide rushes in, the stakes continue to rise. If the Blackout team fails, it's not just Lantern Beach at stake—it's the whole country. Can Benjamin and CJ overcome their differences and work together to find the truth?

Get your copy HERE!

ALSO BY CHRISTY BARRITT:

OTHER BOOKS IN THE LANTERN BEACH UNIVERSE:

LANTERN BEACH MYSTERIES

You can take the detective out of the investigation, but you can't take the investigator out of the detective. A notorious gang puts a bounty on Detective Cady Matthews's head after she takes down their leader, leaving her no choice but to hide until she can testify at trial. But her temporary home across the country on a remote North Carolina island isn't as peaceful as she initially thinks. Living under the new identity of Cassidy Livingston, she struggles to keep her investigative skills tucked away. Can she bring justice to the island . . . or will the hidden currents surrounding her pull her under for good?

Hidden Currents
Flood Watch
Storm Surge
Dangerous Waters
Perilous Riptide
Deadly Undertow

LANTERN BEACH PD

When Cassidy Chambers accepted the job as police chief on Lantern Beach, she knew the island had its secrets. But a mysterious group that's moved onto the island will test all her skills. Cassidy enlists the help of her husband, former Navy SEAL Ty Chambers. Not everything is as it seems, and, as facts materialize, danger on the island grows. Can Cassidy and Ty discover the truth about the shadowy crimes in their cozy community? Or has darkness permanently invaded their beloved Lantern Beach?

On the Lookout
Attempt to Locate
First Degree Murder
Dead on Arrival
Plan of Action

YOU MIGHT ALSO ENJOY ...

THE SQUEAKY CLEAN MYSTERY SERIES

On her way to completing a degree in forensic science, Gabby St. Claire drops out of school and starts her own crime-scene cleaning business. When a routine cleaning job uncovers a murder weapon the police overlooked, she realizes that the wrong person is in jail. She also realizes that crime scene cleaning might be the perfect career for utilizing her investigative skills.

#1 Hazardous Duty
#2 Suspicious Minds
#2.5 It Came Upon a Midnight Crime (novella)
#3 Organized Grime
#4 Dirty Deeds
#5 The Scum of All Fears

#6 To Love, Honor and Perish

#7 Mucky Streak

#8 Foul Play

#9 Broom & Gloom

#10 Dust and Obey

#11 Thrill Squeaker

#11.5 Swept Away (novella)

#12 Cunning Attractions

#13 Cold Case: Clean Getaway

#14 Cold Case: Clean Sweep

#15 Cold Case: Clean Break

While You Were Sweeping, A Riley Thomas Spinoff

THE WORST DETECTIVE EVER:

I'm not really a private detective. I just play one on TV.

Joey Darling, better known to the world as Raven Remington, detective extraordinaire, is trying to separate herself from her invincible alter ego. She played the spunky character for five years on the hit TV show *Relentless*, which catapulted her to fame and into the role of Hollywood's sweetheart. When her marriage falls apart, her finances dwindle to nothing, and her father disappears, Joey finds herself on the Outer Banks of North Carolina, trying to piece together her life away from the limelight. But as people continually mistake her for the character she played on TV, she's tasked with solving real life crimes ... even though she's terrible at it.

#1 Ready to Fumble
#2 Reign of Error
#3 Safety in Blunders
#4 Join the Flub
#5 Blooper Freak
#6 Flaw Abiding Citizen
#7 Gaffe Out Loud
#8 Joke and Dagger
#9 Wreck the Halls
#10 Glitch and Famous (coming soon)

ABOUT THE AUTHOR

USA Today has called Christy Barritt's books "scary, funny, passionate, and quirky."

Christy writes both mystery and romantic suspense novels that are clean with underlying messages of faith. Her books have won the Daphne du Maurier Award for Excellence in Suspense and Mystery, have been twice nominated for the Romantic Times Reviewers' Choice Award, and have finaled for both a Carol Award and Foreword Magazine's Book of the Year. She's a *USA Today* and *Publishers Weekly* Bestseller, and her books have sold more than two million copies.

She is married to her Prince Charming, a man who thinks she's hilarious—but only when she's not trying to be. Christy is a self-proclaimed klutz, an avid music lover who's known for spontaneously bursting into song, and a road trip aficionado.

When she's not working or spending time with her family, she enjoys singing, playing the guitar, and exploring small, unsuspecting towns where people have no idea how accident-prone she is.

Find Christy online at:
- **www.christybarritt.com**
- **www.facebook.com/christybarritt**
- **www.twitter.com/cbarritt**

Sign up for Christy's newsletter to get information on all of her latest releases here: **www.christybarritt.com/newsletter-sign-up/**

If you enjoyed this book, please consider leaving a review.

Made in the USA
Monee, IL
04 July 2021